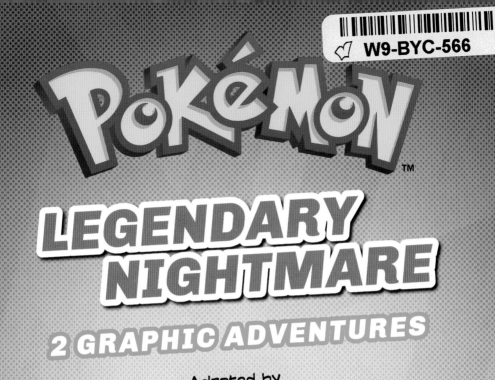

POKÉMON™

LEGENDARY NIGHTMARE

2 GRAPHIC ADVENTURES

Adapted by
Meredith Rusu

graphix
An Imprint of
SCHOLASTIC

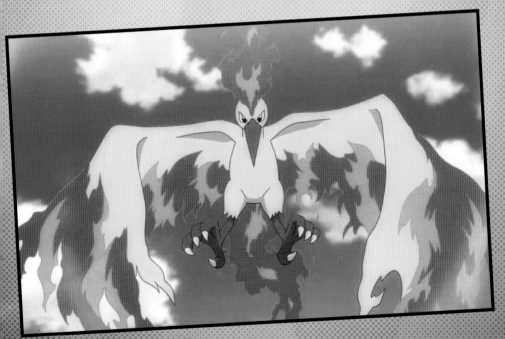

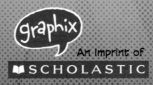

ISBN 978-1-338-87138-8

10 9 8 7 6 5 4 3 2 1   23 24 25 26 27

Designed by Cheung Tai

Printed in China   62

First printing 2023

CONTENTS

Story 1
Fire-Type Feud

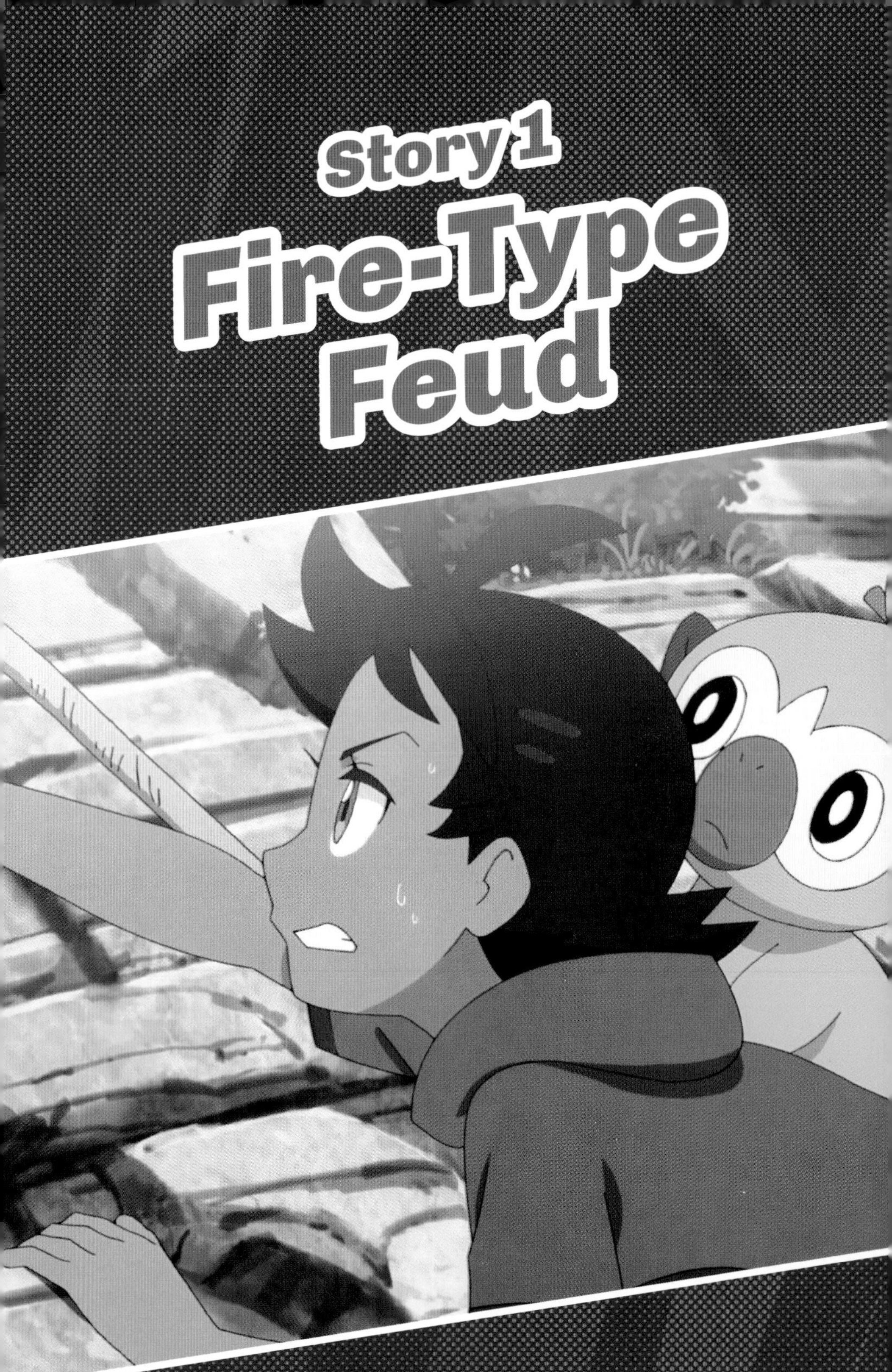

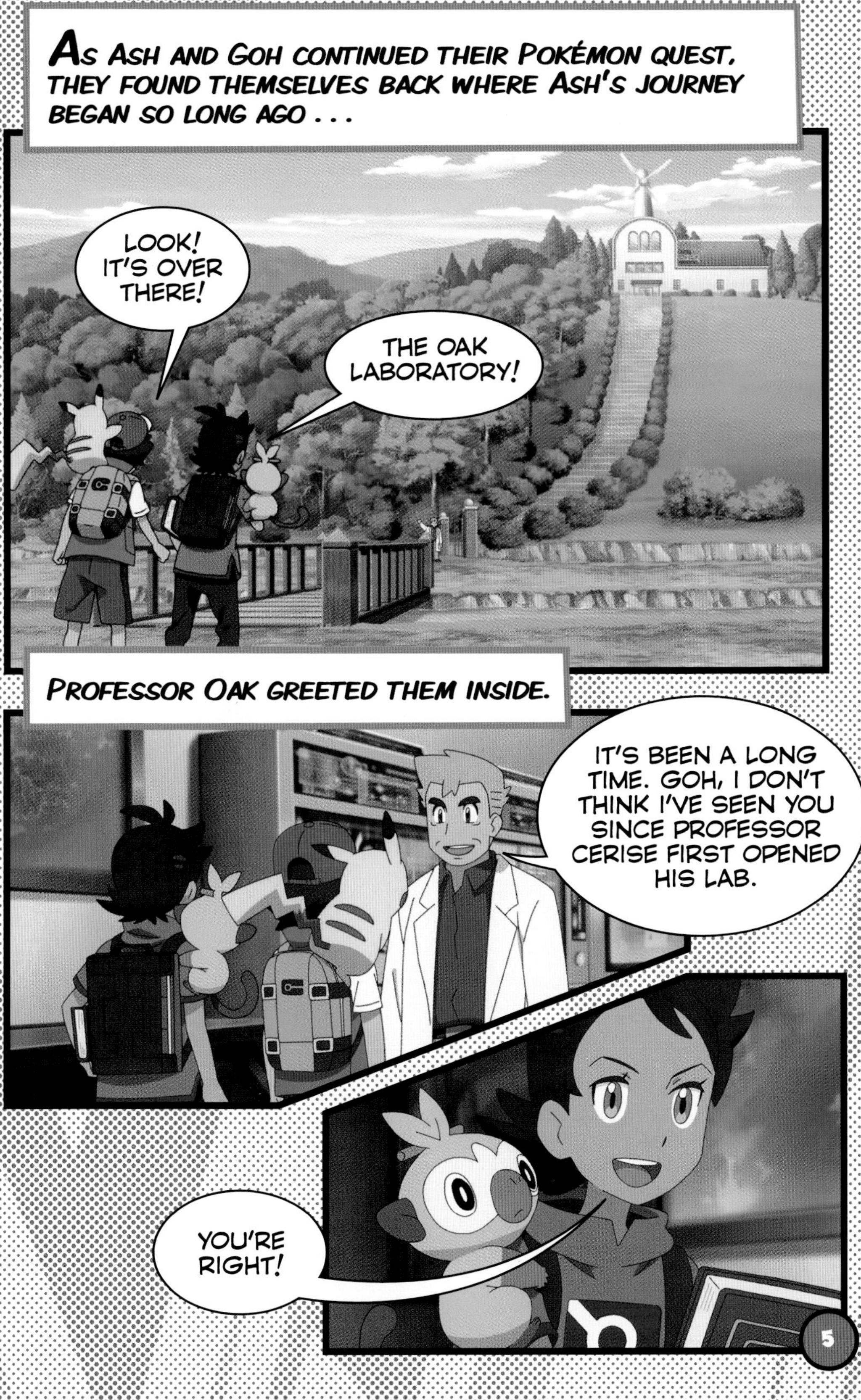
AS ASH AND GOH CONTINUED THEIR POKÉMON QUEST, THEY FOUND THEMSELVES BACK WHERE ASH'S JOURNEY BEGAN SO LONG AGO . . .
LOOK! IT'S OVER THERE!
THE OAK LABORATORY!
PROFESSOR OAK GREETED THEM INSIDE.
IT'S BEEN A LONG TIME. GOH, I DON'T THINK I'VE SEEN YOU SINCE PROFESSOR CERISE FIRST OPENED HIS LAB.
YOU'RE RIGHT!

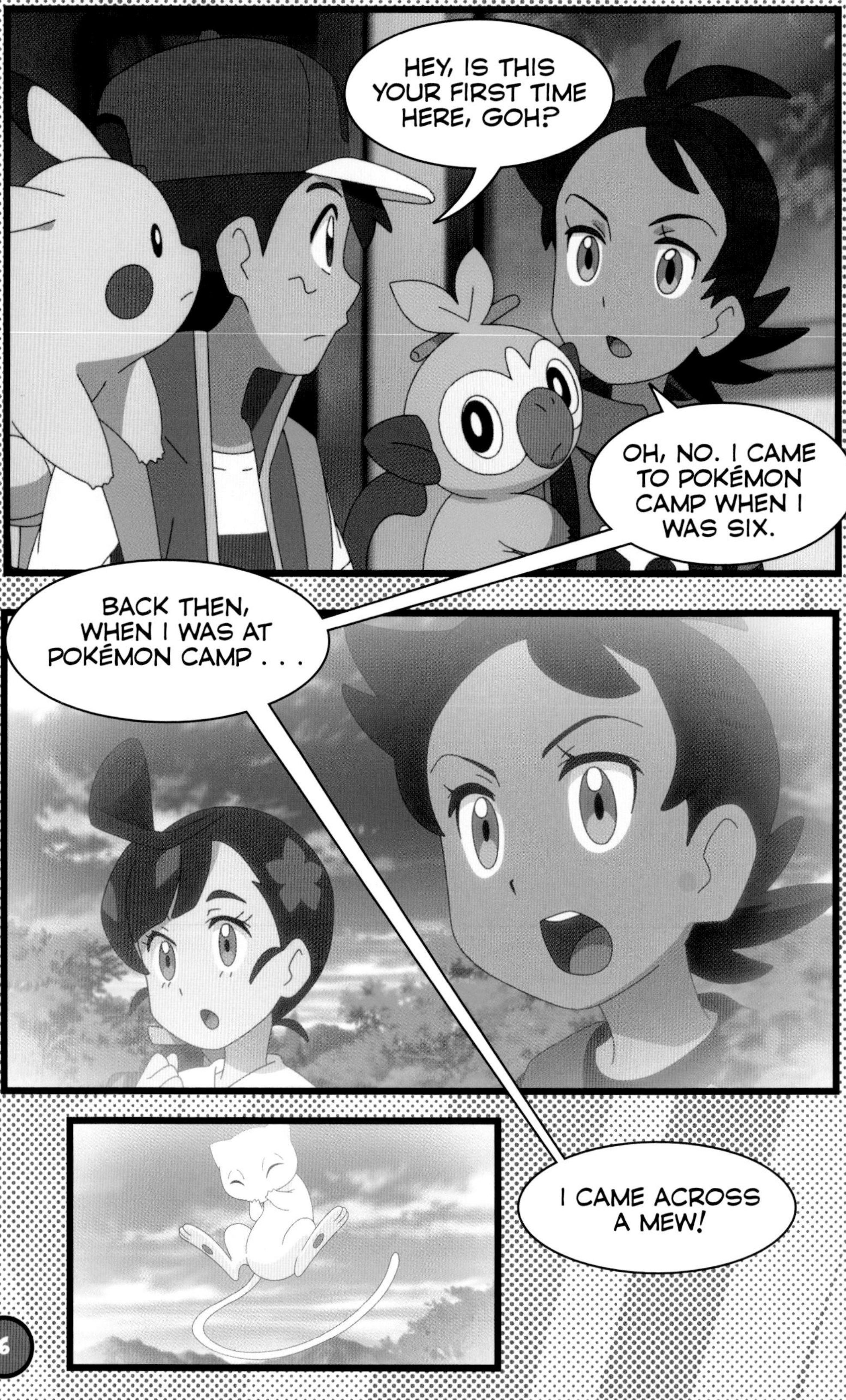
HEY, IS THIS YOUR FIRST TIME HERE, GOH?
OH, NO. I CAME TO POKÉMON CAMP WHEN I WAS SIX.
BACK THEN, WHEN I WAS AT POKÉMON CAMP . . .
I CAME ACROSS A MEW!

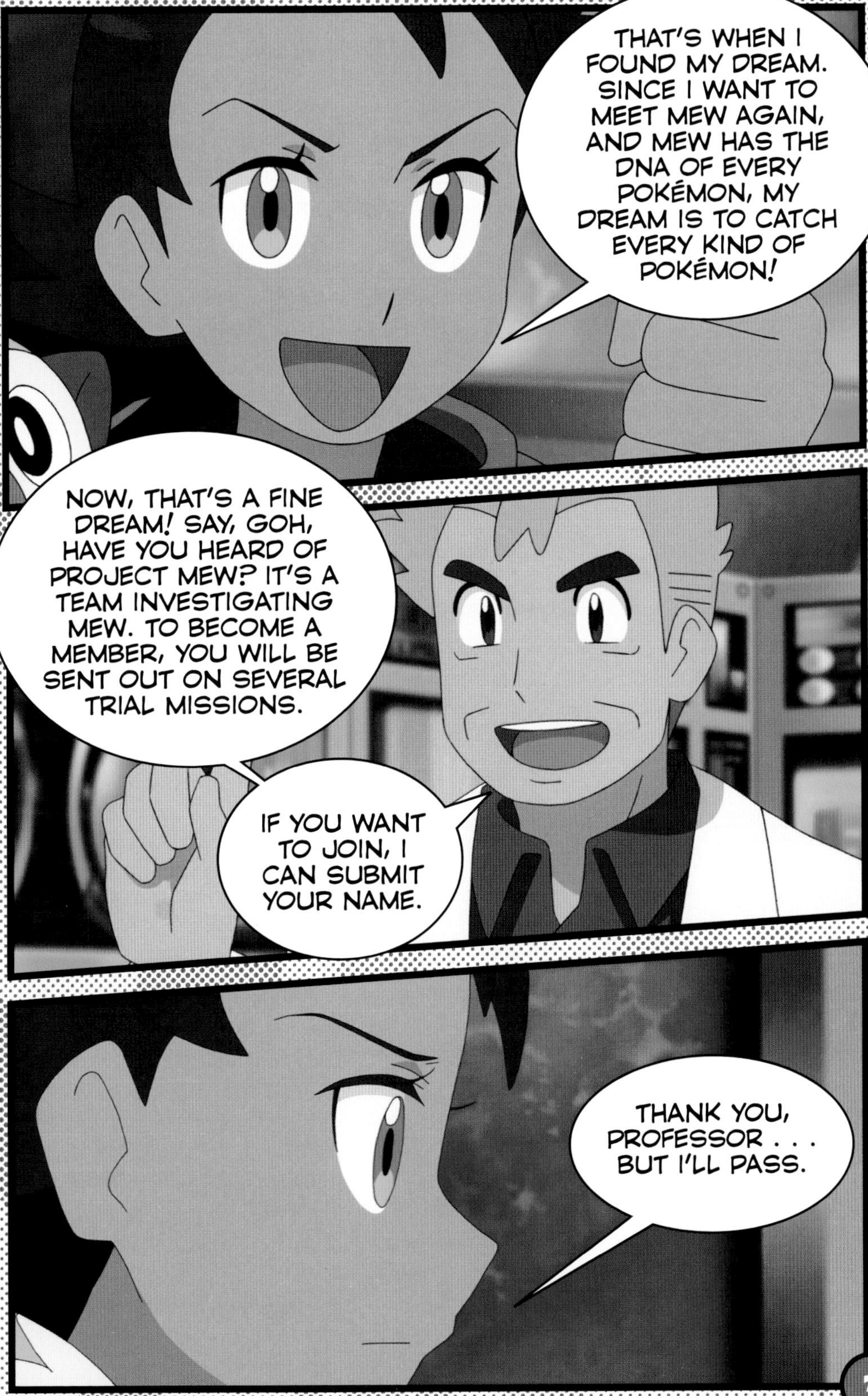
THAT'S WHEN I FOUND MY DREAM. SINCE I WANT TO MEET MEW AGAIN, AND MEW HAS THE DNA OF EVERY POKÉMON, MY DREAM IS TO CATCH EVERY KIND OF POKÉMON!
NOW, THAT'S A FINE DREAM! SAY, GOH, HAVE YOU HEARD OF PROJECT MEW? IT'S A TEAM INVESTIGATING MEW. TO BECOME A MEMBER, YOU WILL BE SENT OUT ON SEVERAL TRIAL MISSIONS.
IF YOU WANT TO JOIN, I CAN SUBMIT YOUR NAME.
THANK YOU, PROFESSOR . . . BUT I'LL PASS.

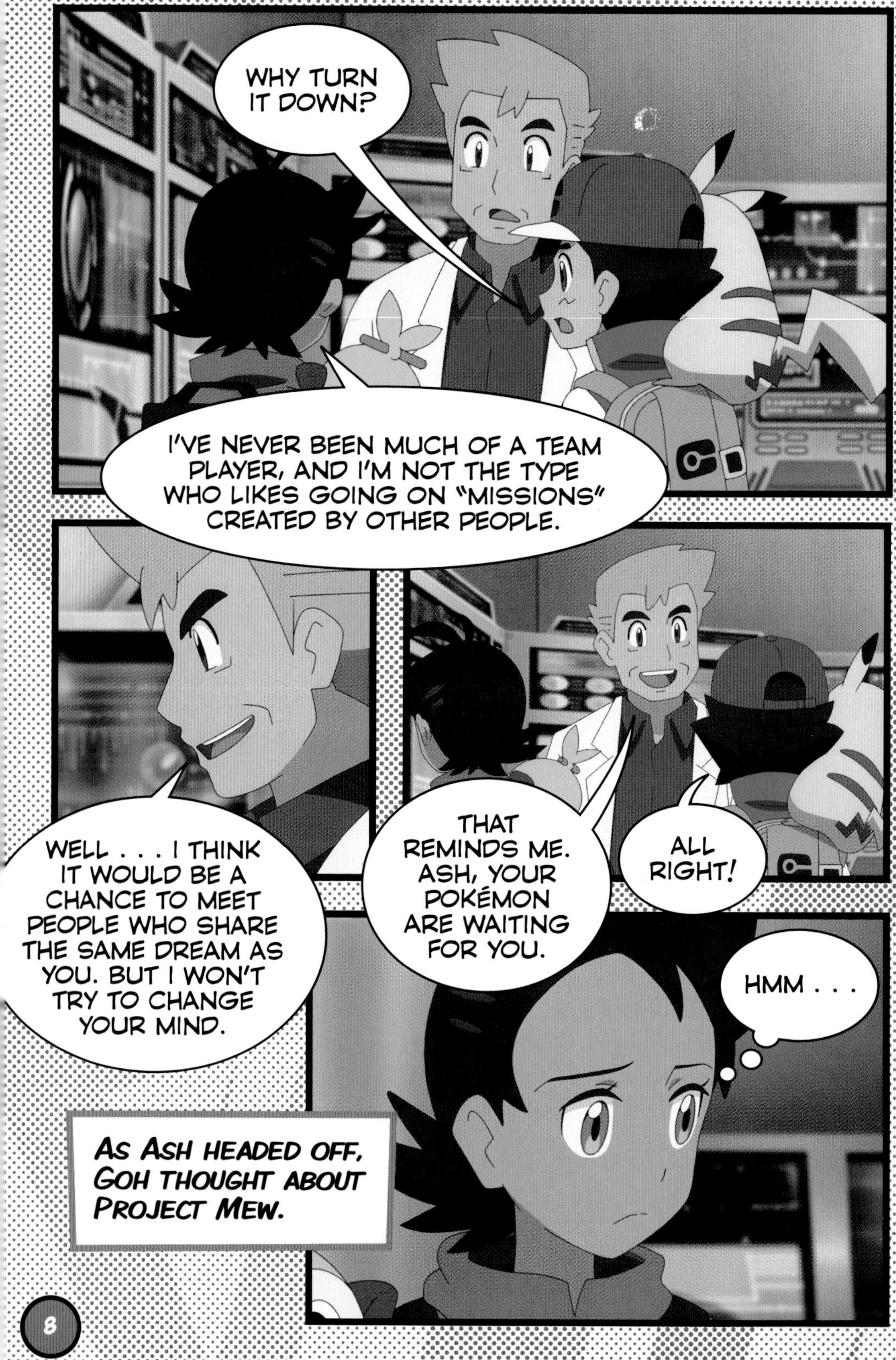
WHY TURN IT DOWN?
I'VE NEVER BEEN MUCH OF A TEAM PLAYER, AND I'M NOT THE TYPE WHO LIKES GOING ON "MISSIONS" CREATED BY OTHER PEOPLE.
WELL . . . I THINK IT WOULD BE A CHANCE TO MEET PEOPLE WHO SHARE THE SAME DREAM AS YOU. BUT I WON'T TRY TO CHANGE YOUR MIND.
THAT REMINDS ME. ASH, YOUR POKÉMON ARE WAITING FOR YOU.
ALL RIGHT!
HMM . . .
AS ASH HEADED OFF, GOH THOUGHT ABOUT PROJECT MEW.

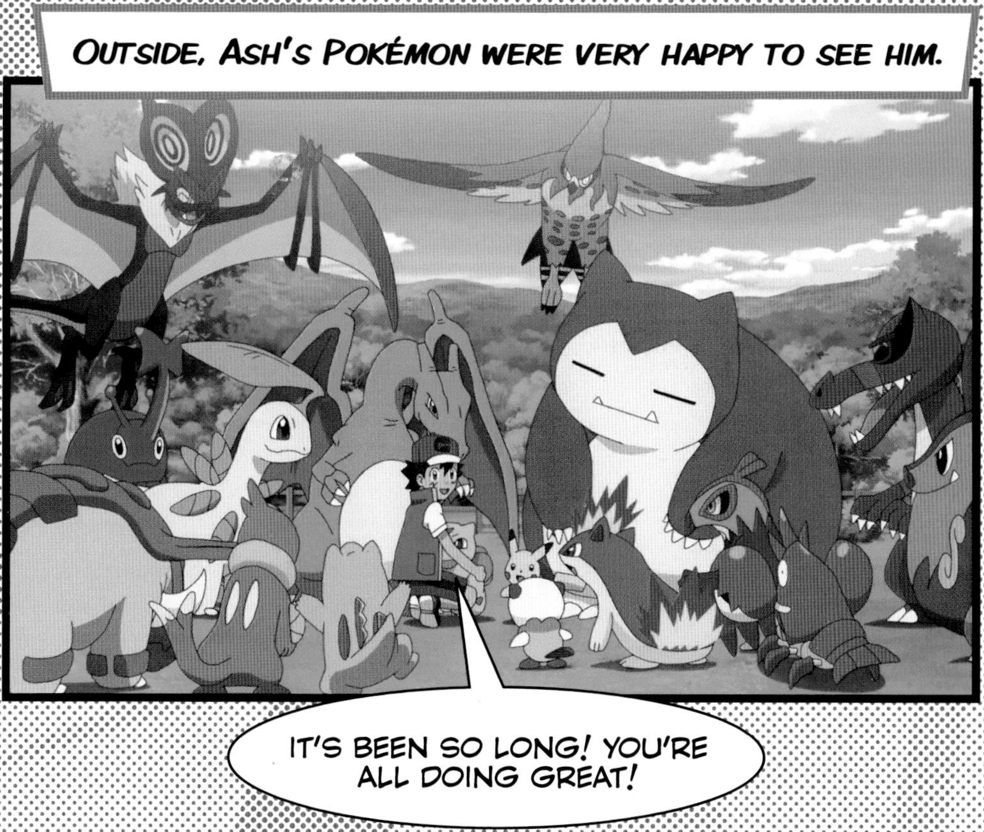
OUTSIDE, ASH'S POKÉMON WERE VERY HAPPY TO SEE HIM.
IT'S BEEN SO LONG! YOU'RE ALL DOING GREAT!

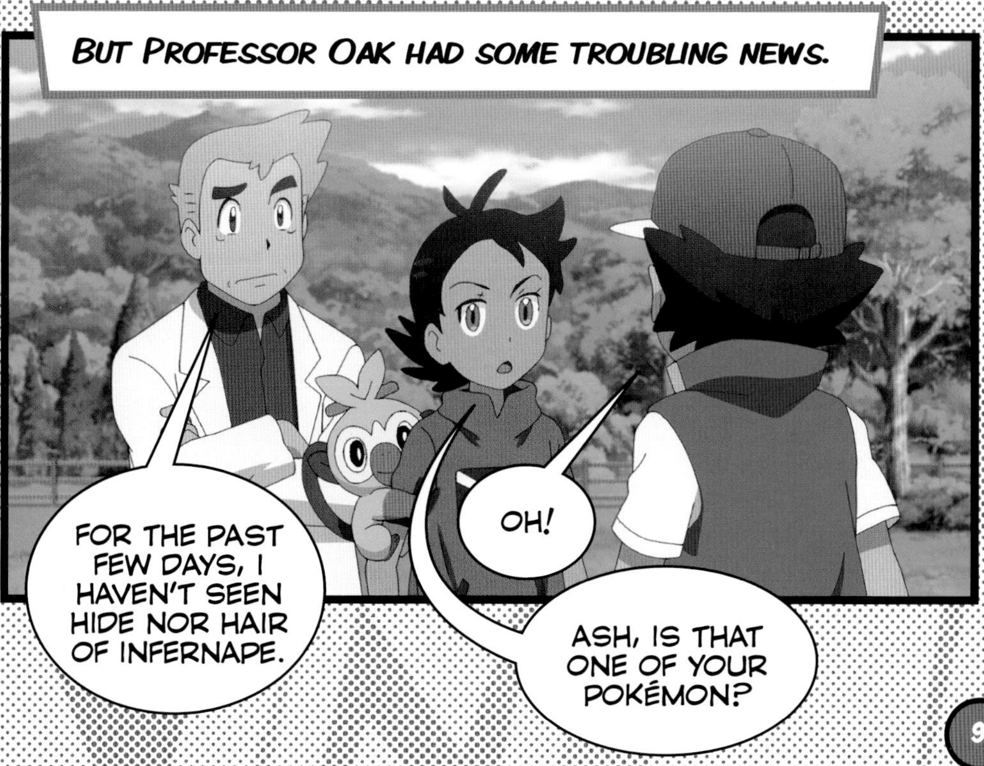
BUT PROFESSOR OAK HAD SOME TROUBLING NEWS.
FOR THE PAST FEW DAYS, I HAVEN'T SEEN HIDE NOR HAIR OF INFERNAPE.
OH!
ASH, IS THAT ONE OF YOUR POKÉMON?

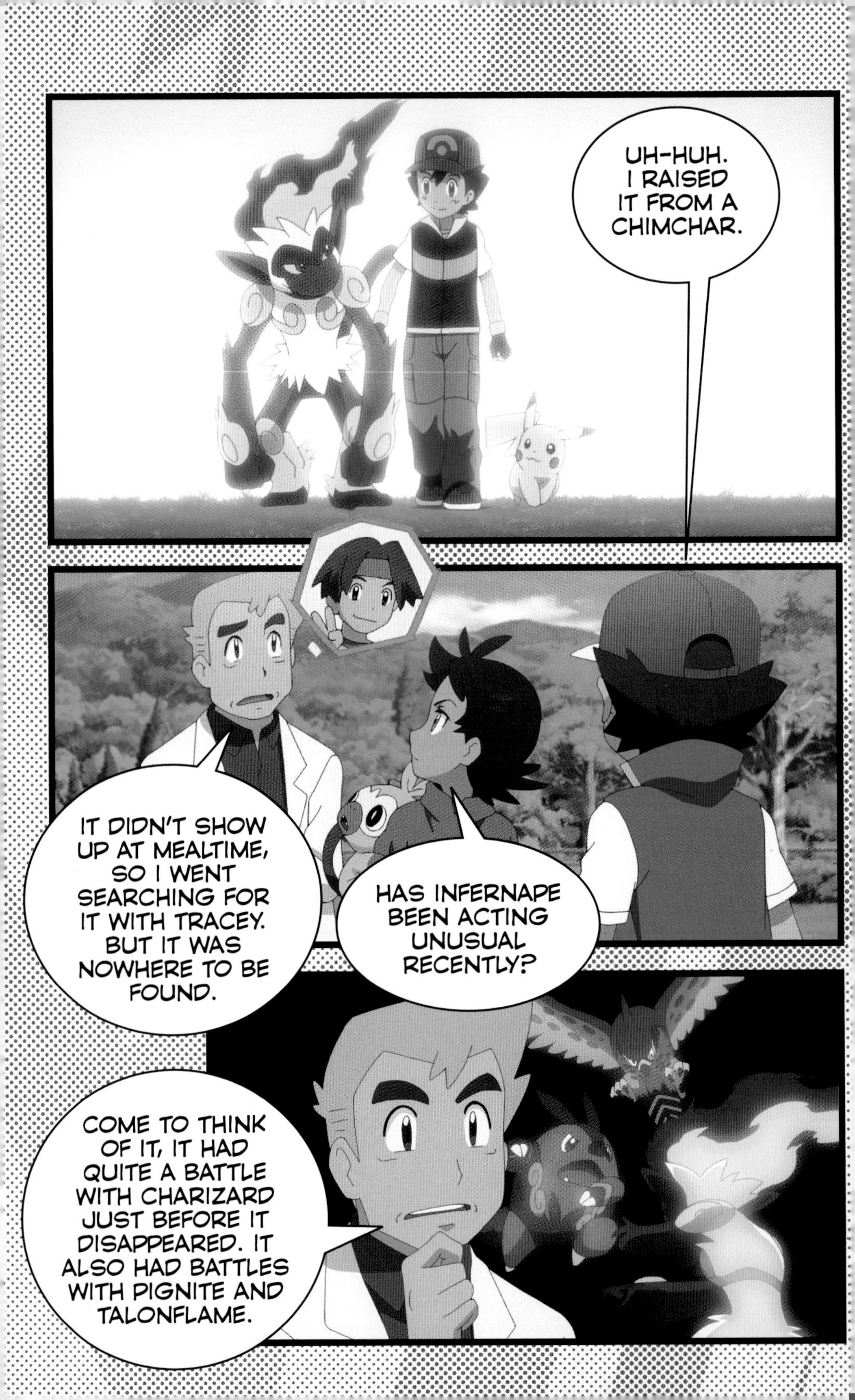
UH-HUH. I RAISED IT FROM A CHIMCHAR.
HAS INFERNAPE BEEN ACTING UNUSUAL RECENTLY?
IT DIDN'T SHOW UP AT MEALTIME, SO I WENT SEARCHING FOR IT WITH TRACEY. BUT IT WAS NOWHERE TO BE FOUND.
COME TO THINK OF IT, IT HAD QUITE A BATTLE WITH CHARIZARD JUST BEFORE IT DISAPPEARED. IT ALSO HAD BATTLES WITH PIGNITE AND TALONFLAME.

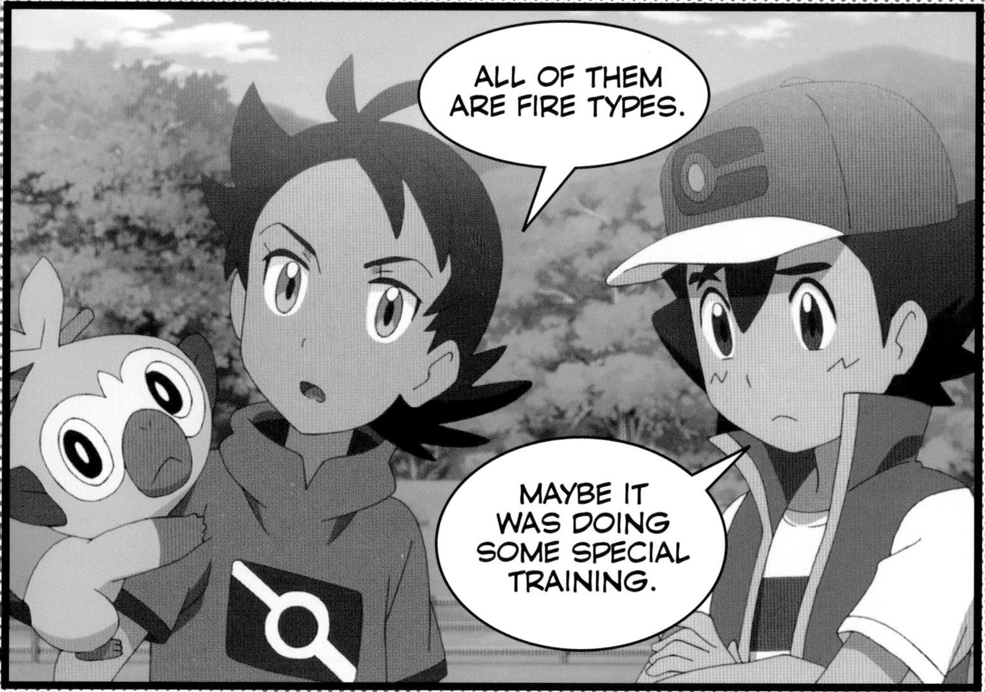
ALL OF THEM ARE FIRE TYPES.
MAYBE IT WAS DOING SOME SPECIAL TRAINING.

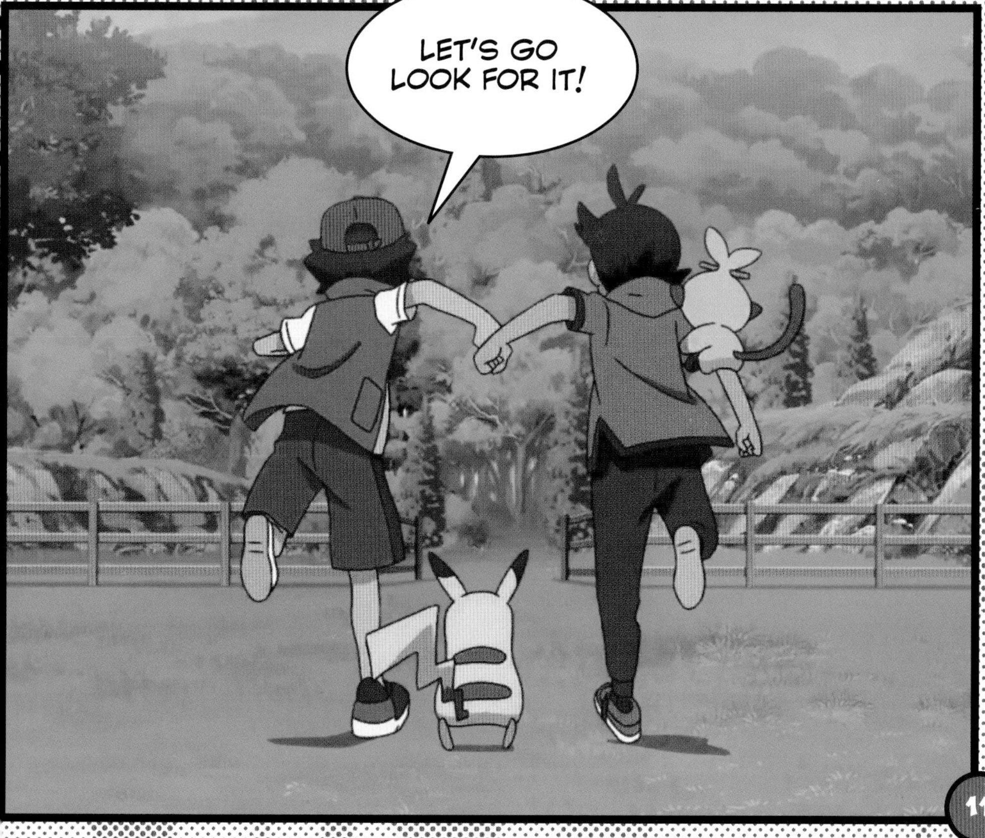
LET'S GO LOOK FOR IT!

As Ash and Goh searched the forest for Infernape, they found something else instead . . .

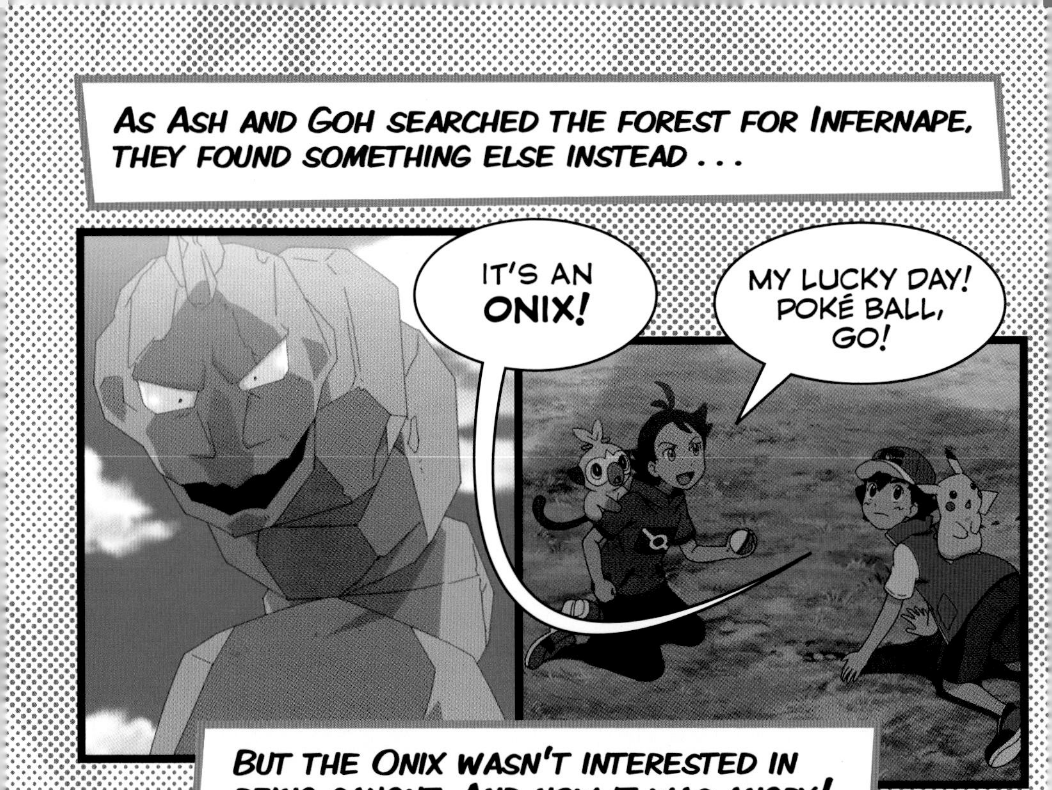
It's an Onix!
My lucky day! Poké Ball, go!

But the Onix wasn't interested in being caught. And now it was angry!

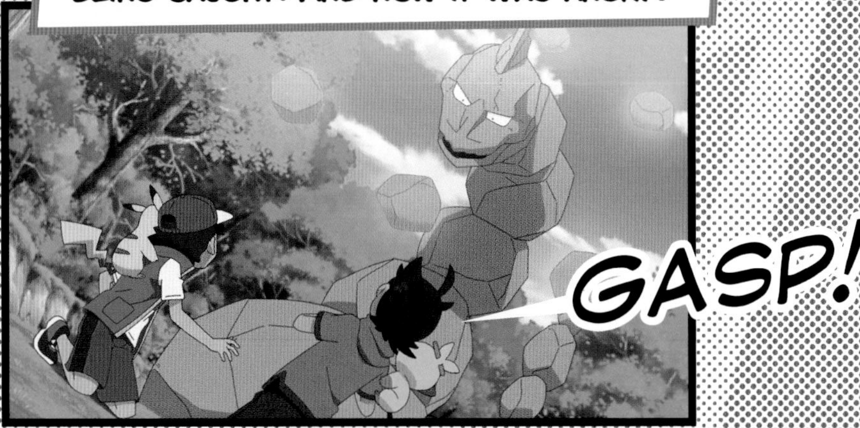
GASP!

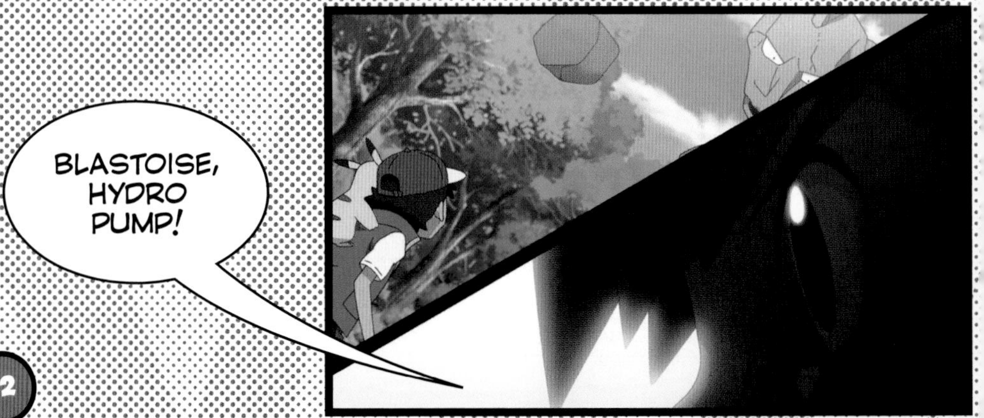
Blastoise, Hydro Pump!

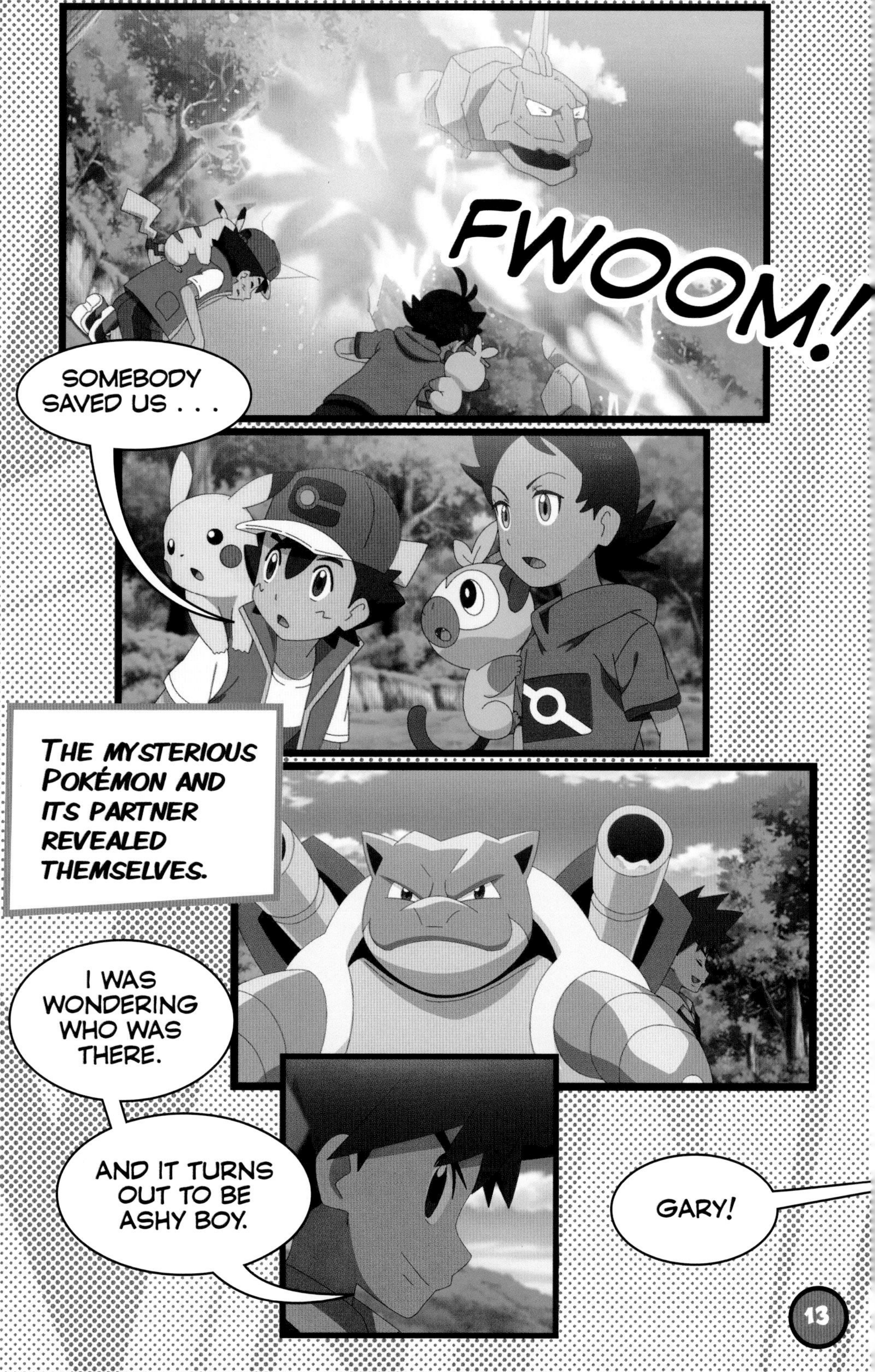
FWOOM!
SOMEBODY SAVED US . . .
THE MYSTERIOUS POKÉMON AND ITS PARTNER REVEALED THEMSELVES.
I WAS WONDERING WHO WAS THERE.
AND IT TURNS OUT TO BE ASHY BOY.
GARY!

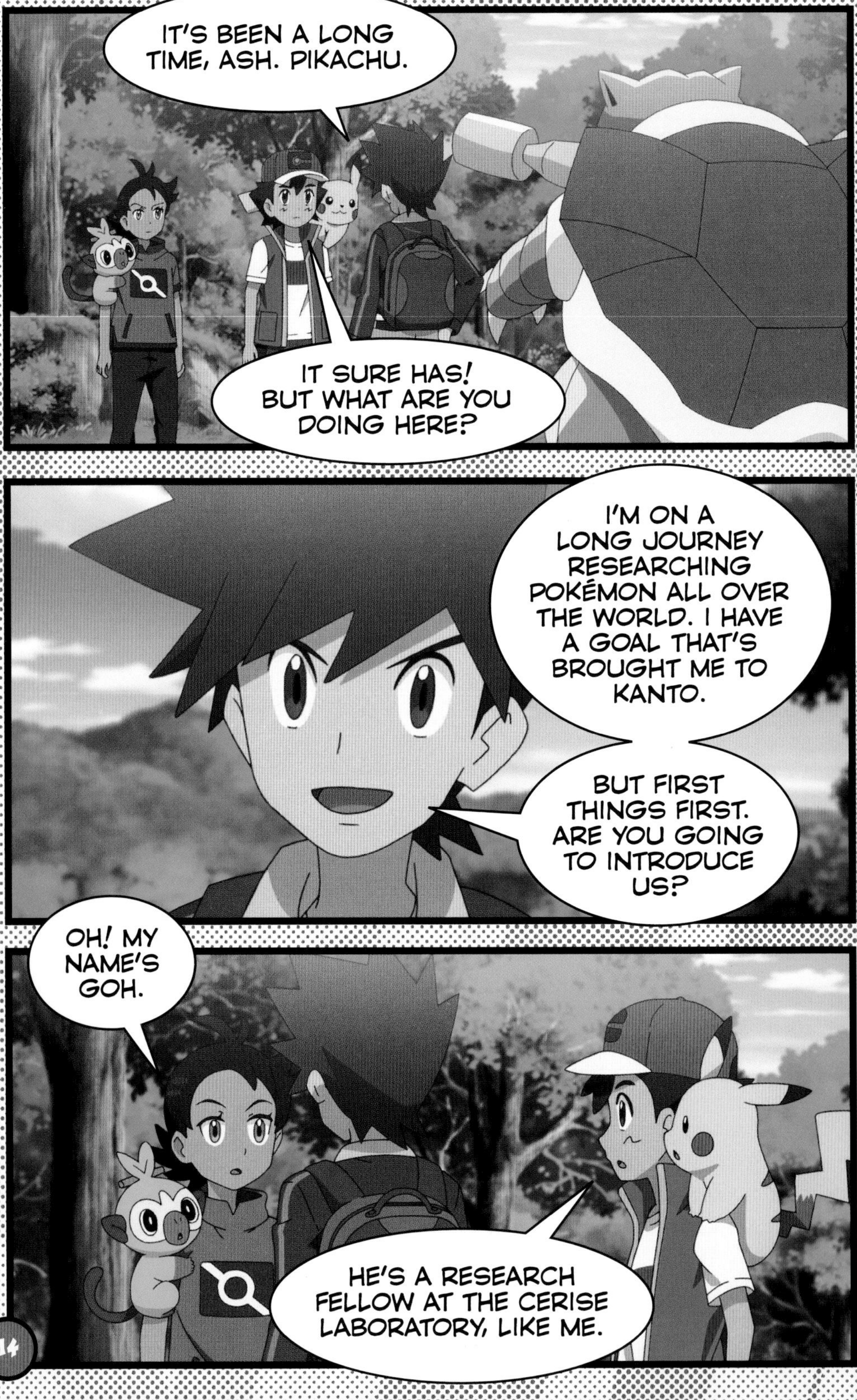
IT'S BEEN A LONG TIME, ASH. PIKACHU.
IT SURE HAS! BUT WHAT ARE YOU DOING HERE?
I'M ON A LONG JOURNEY RESEARCHING POKÉMON ALL OVER THE WORLD. I HAVE A GOAL THAT'S BROUGHT ME TO KANTO.
BUT FIRST THINGS FIRST. ARE YOU GOING TO INTRODUCE US?
OH! MY NAME'S GOH.
HE'S A RESEARCH FELLOW AT THE CERISE LABORATORY, LIKE ME.

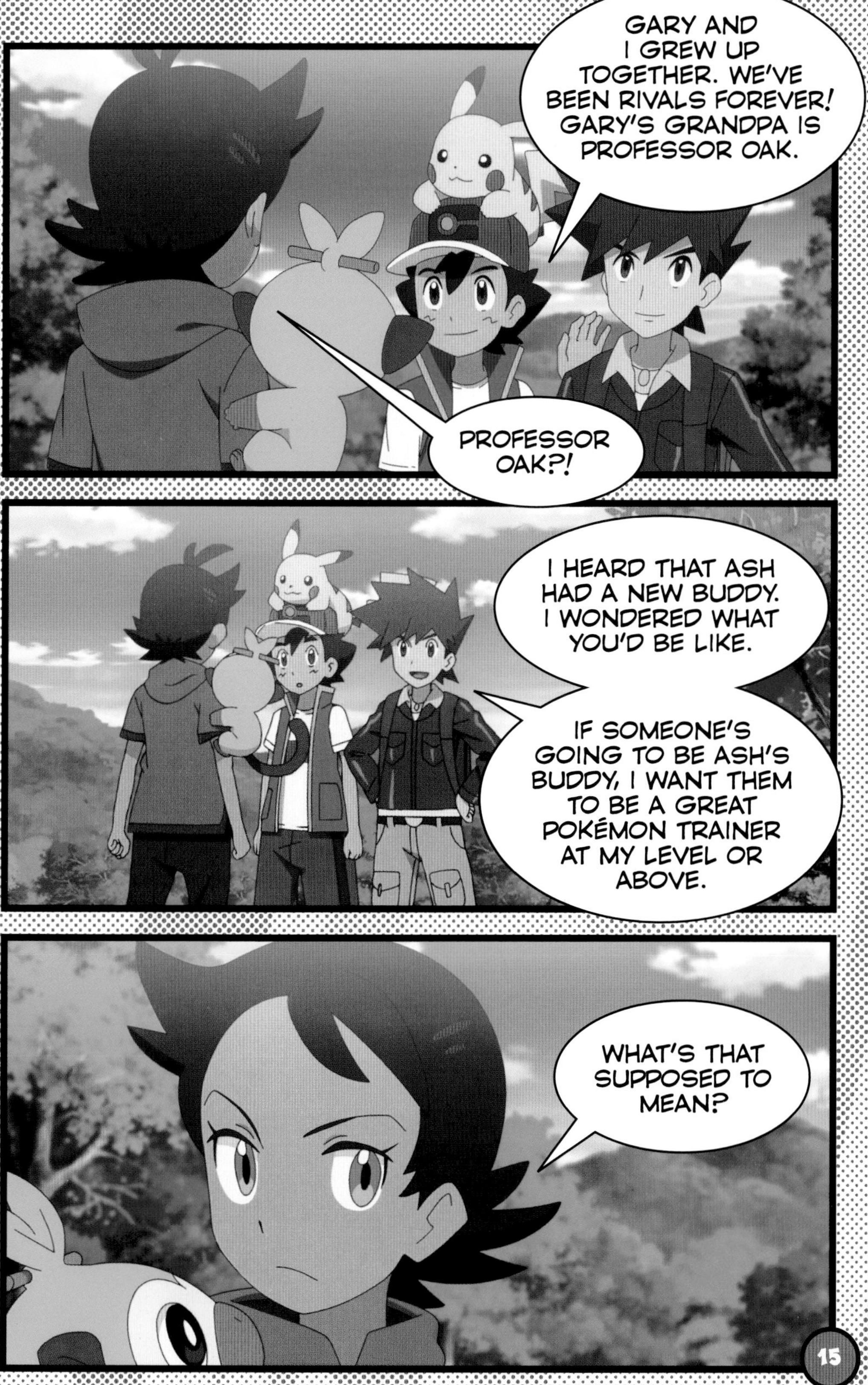
GARY AND I GREW UP TOGETHER. WE'VE BEEN RIVALS FOREVER! GARY'S GRANDPA IS PROFESSOR OAK.
PROFESSOR OAK?!
I HEARD THAT ASH HAD A NEW BUDDY. I WONDERED WHAT YOU'D BE LIKE.
IF SOMEONE'S GOING TO BE ASH'S BUDDY, I WANT THEM TO BE A GREAT POKÉMON TRAINER AT MY LEVEL OR ABOVE.
WHAT'S THAT SUPPOSED TO MEAN?

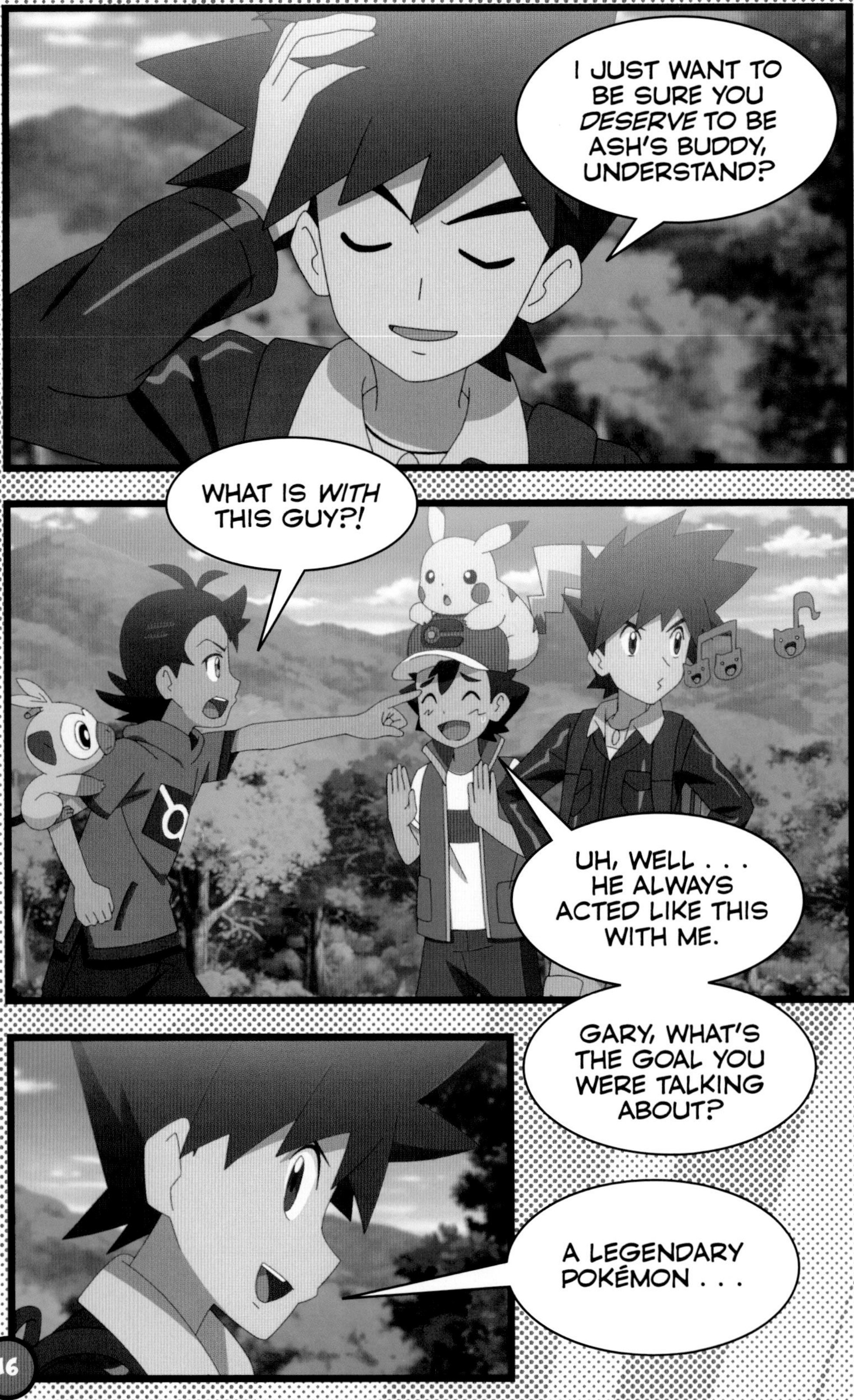
I JUST WANT TO BE SURE YOU *DESERVE* TO BE ASH'S BUDDY, UNDERSTAND?
WHAT IS *WITH* THIS GUY?!
UH, WELL . . . HE ALWAYS ACTED LIKE THIS WITH ME.
GARY, WHAT'S THE GOAL YOU WERE TALKING ABOUT?
A LEGENDARY POKÉMON . . .

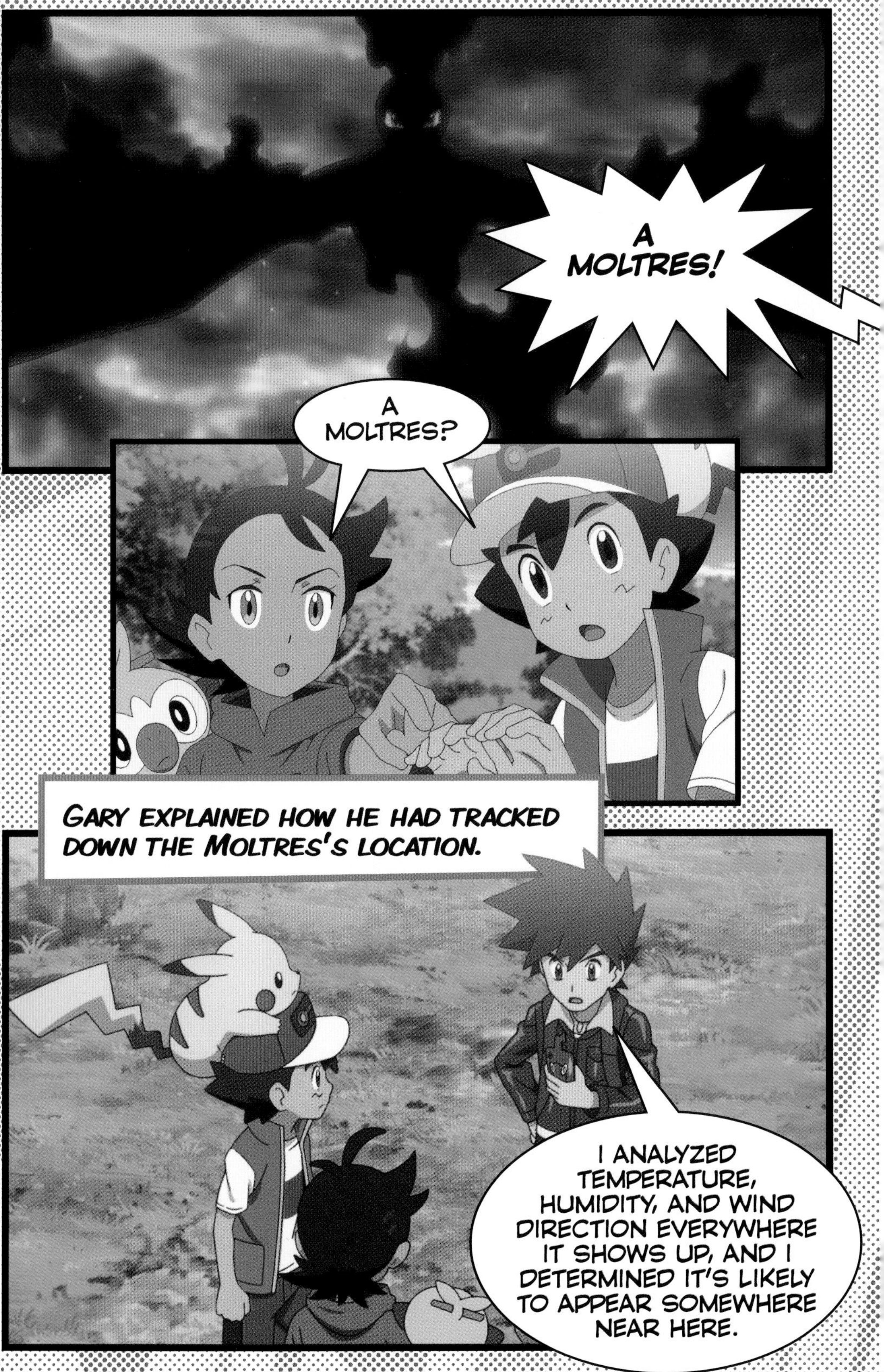
A MOLTRES!
A MOLTRES?
GARY EXPLAINED HOW HE HAD TRACKED DOWN THE MOLTRES'S LOCATION.
I ANALYZED TEMPERATURE, HUMIDITY, AND WIND DIRECTION EVERYWHERE IT SHOWS UP, AND I DETERMINED IT'S LIKELY TO APPEAR SOMEWHERE NEAR HERE.

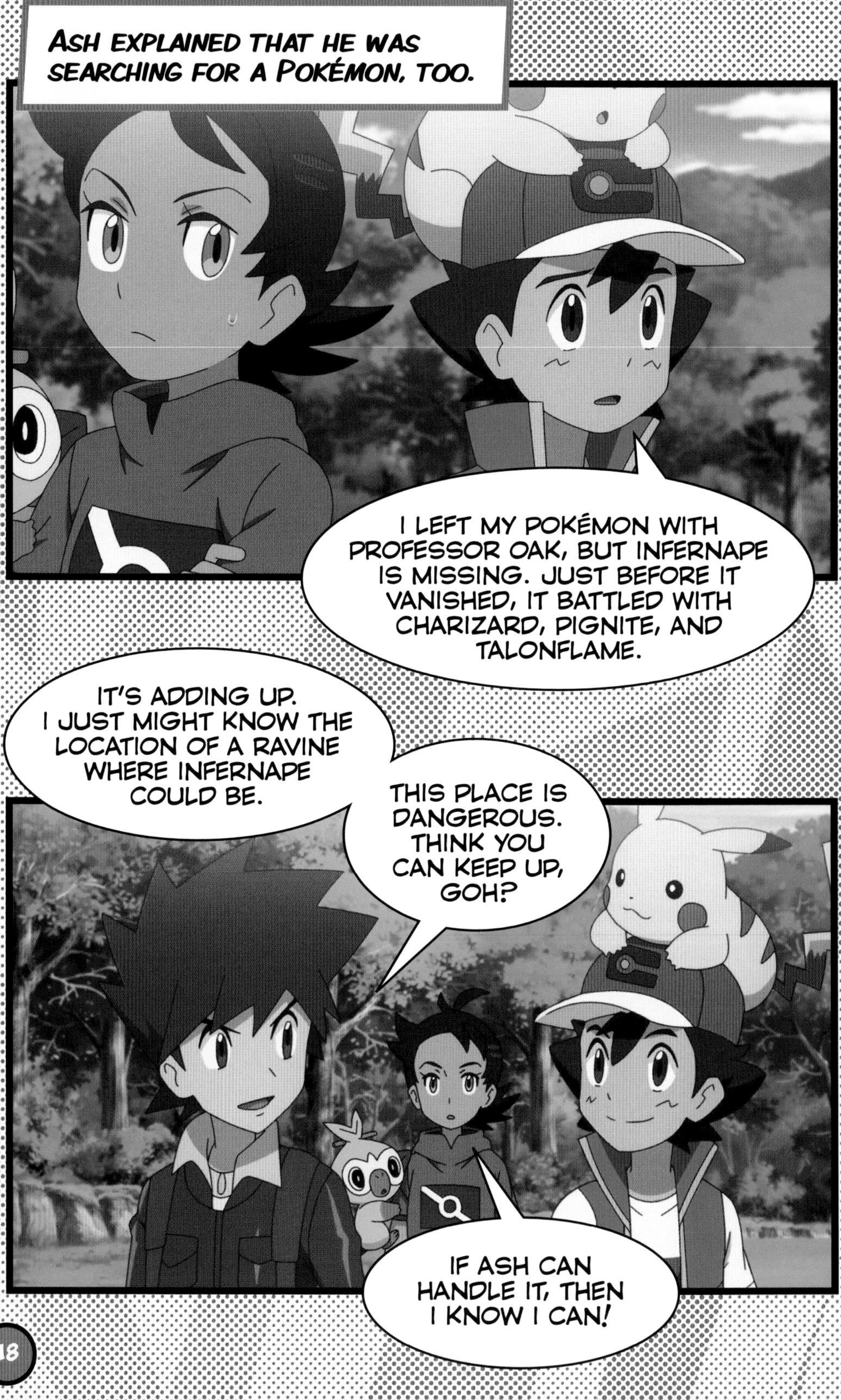
ASH EXPLAINED THAT HE WAS SEARCHING FOR A POKÉMON, TOO.
I LEFT MY POKÉMON WITH PROFESSOR OAK, BUT INFERNAPE IS MISSING. JUST BEFORE IT VANISHED, IT BATTLED WITH CHARIZARD, PIGNITE, AND TALONFLAME.
IT'S ADDING UP. I JUST MIGHT KNOW THE LOCATION OF A RAVINE WHERE INFERNAPE COULD BE.
THIS PLACE IS DANGEROUS. THINK YOU CAN KEEP UP, GOH?
IF ASH CAN HANDLE IT, THEN I KNOW I CAN!

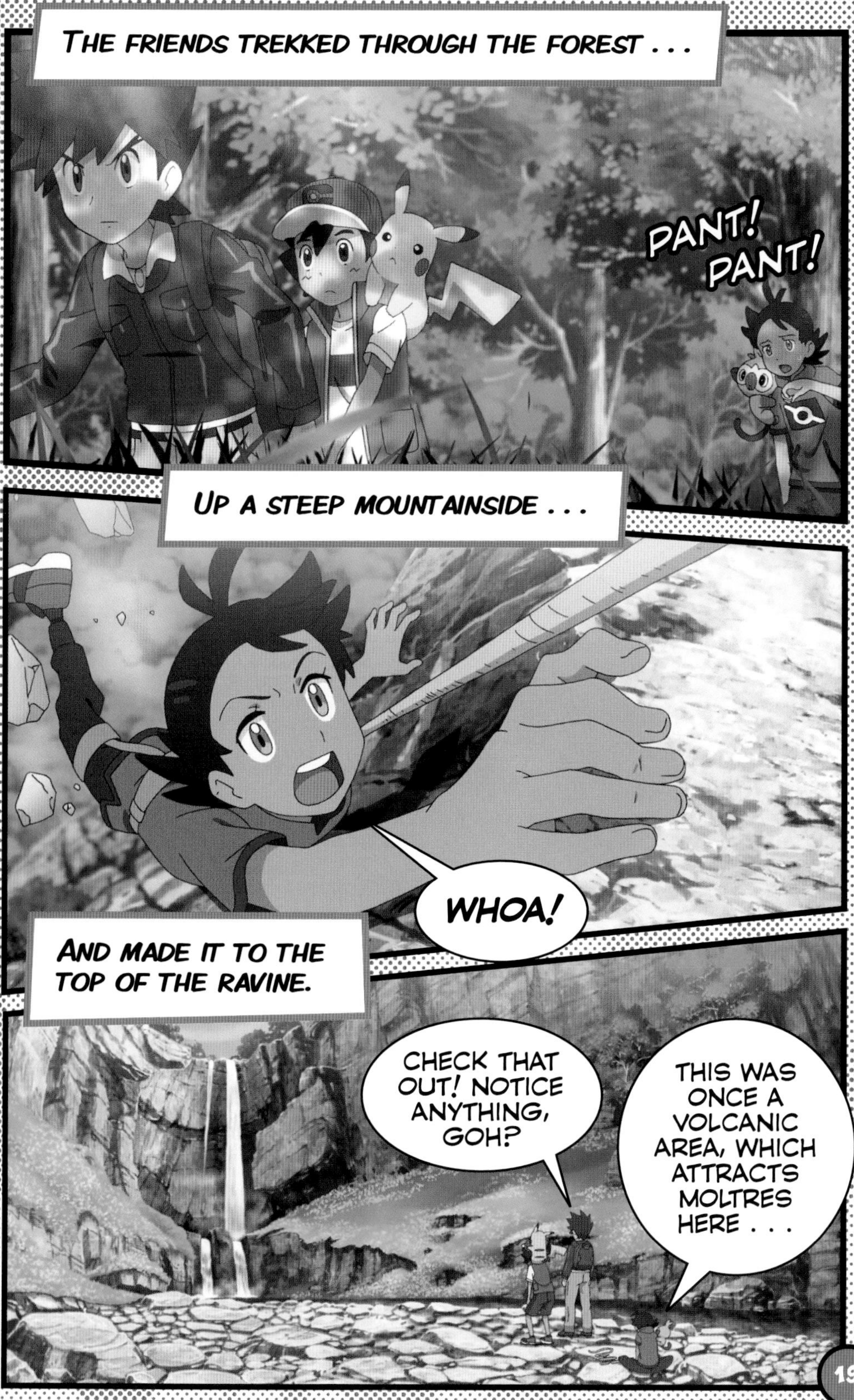
THE FRIENDS TREKKED THROUGH THE FOREST . . .
PANT! PANT!
UP A STEEP MOUNTAINSIDE . . .
WHOA!
AND MADE IT TO THE TOP OF THE RAVINE.
CHECK THAT OUT! NOTICE ANYTHING, GOH?
THIS WAS ONCE A VOLCANIC AREA, WHICH ATTRACTS MOLTRES HERE . . .

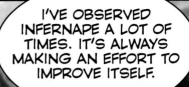

I'VE OBSERVED INFERNAPE A LOT OF TIMES. IT'S ALWAYS MAKING AN EFFORT TO IMPROVE ITSELF.

SO, IF YOUR INFERNAPE WANTED TO CHALLENGE AN EVEN STRONGER POKÉMON TO A BATTLE, IT'S LIKELY IT WANTS THE LEGENDARY FIRE-TYPE MOLTRES AS ITS OPPONENT.

HIGH ABOVE, THE FRIENDS SUDDENLY HEARD INFERNAPE CALLING OUT TO CHALLENGE MOLTRES.

INFERNAAAPE! INFERNAAAPE!

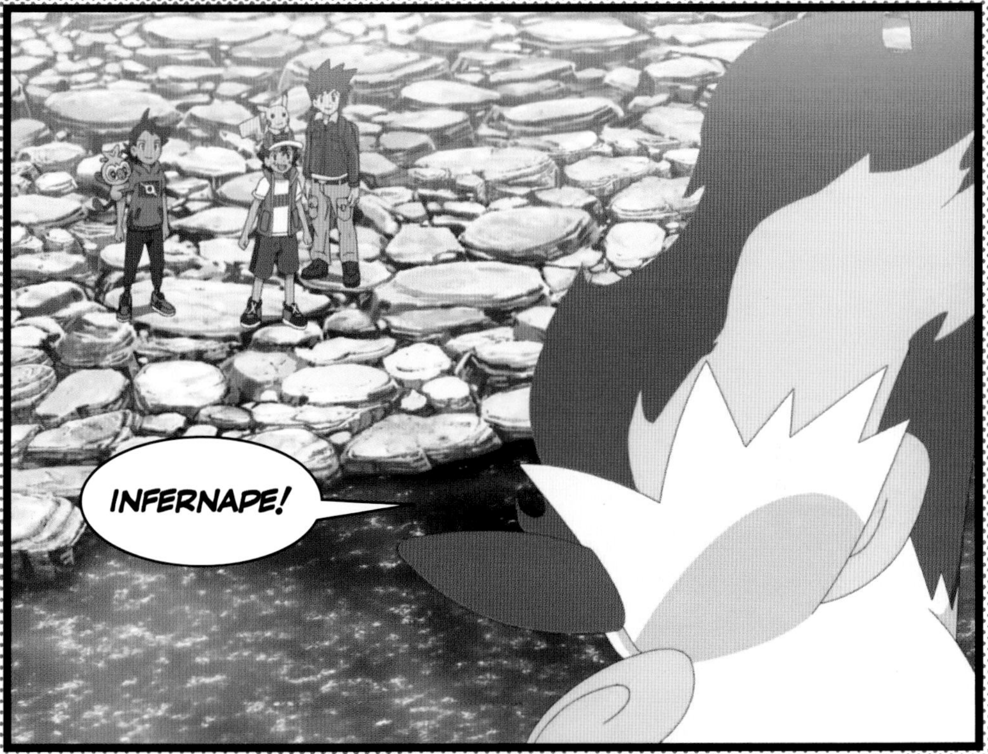
INFERNAPE!

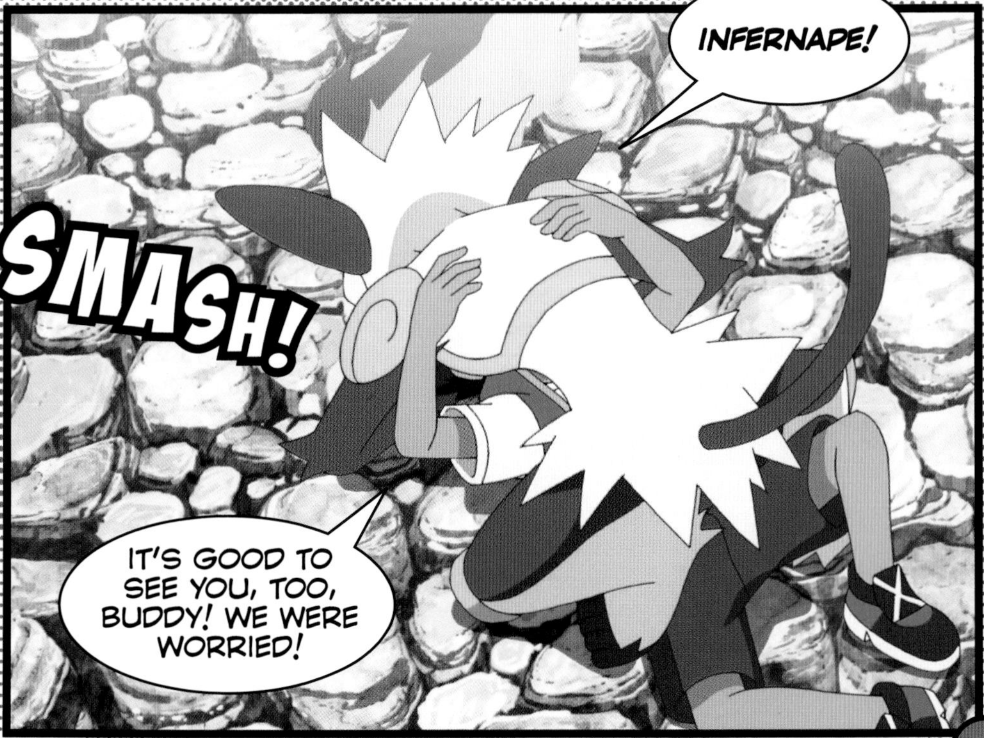
INFERNAPE!
SMASH!
IT'S GOOD TO SEE YOU, TOO, BUDDY! WE WERE WORRIED!

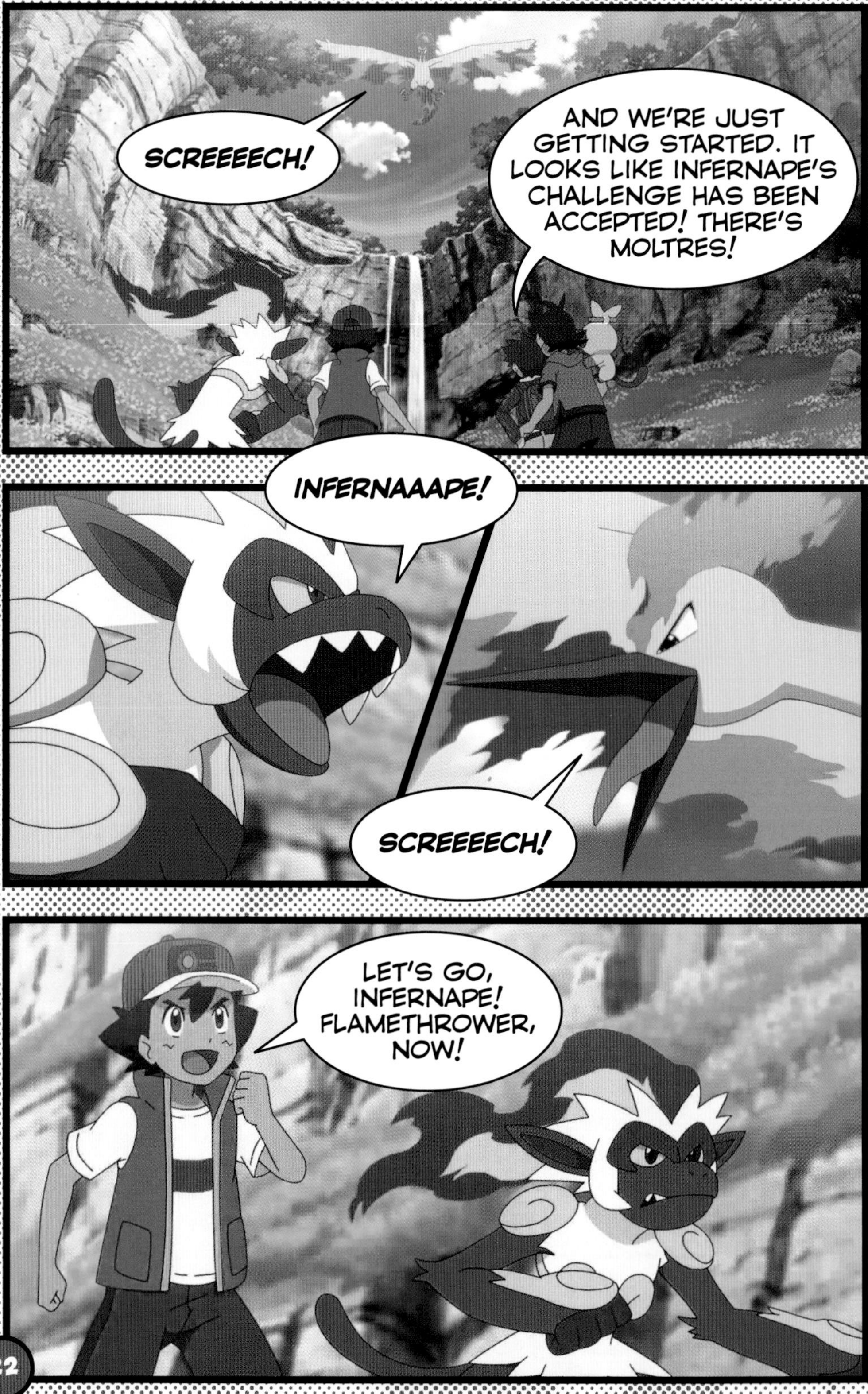
SCREEEECH!
AND WE'RE JUST GETTING STARTED. IT LOOKS LIKE INFERNAPE'S CHALLENGE HAS BEEN ACCEPTED! THERE'S MOLTRES!
INFERNAAAPE!
SCREEEECH!
LET'S GO, INFERNAPE! FLAMETHROWER, NOW!

INFERNAPE LAUNCHED FLAMETHROWER AT MOLTRES.

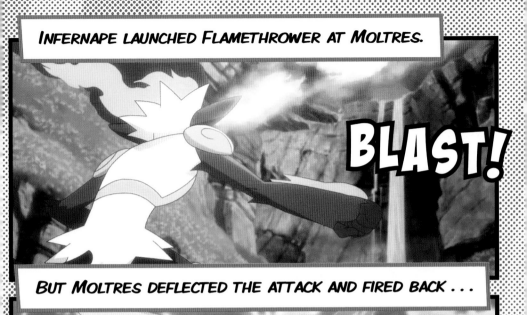

BLAST!

BUT MOLTRES DEFLECTED THE ATTACK AND FIRED BACK . . .

FWOOM!

SURROUNDING INFERNAPE WITH FLAMES!

SIZZZZZZLE!

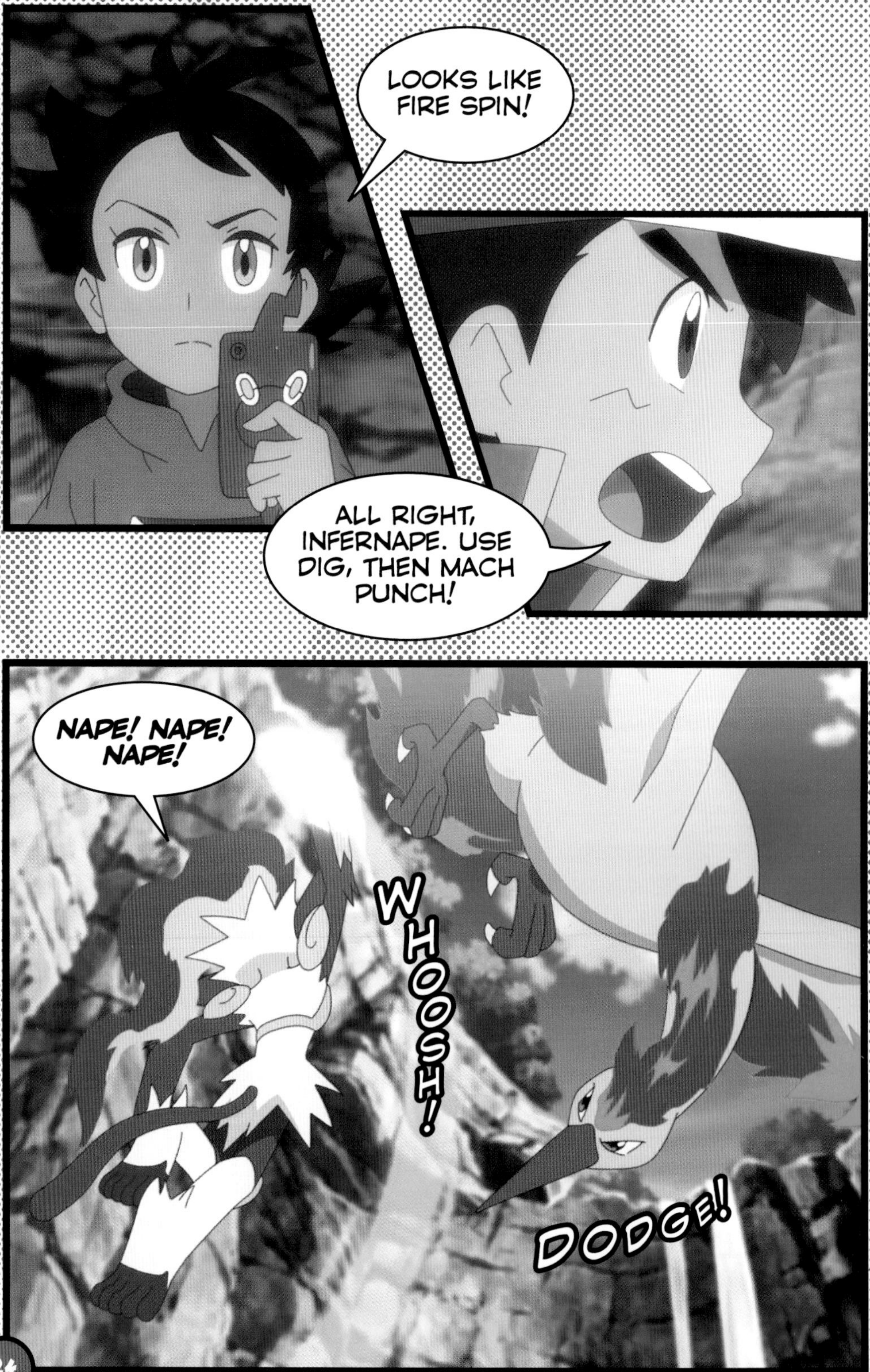
LOOKS LIKE FIRE SPIN!
ALL RIGHT, INFERNAPE. USE DIG, THEN MACH PUNCH!
NAPE! NAPE! NAPE!
WHOOSH!
DODGE!

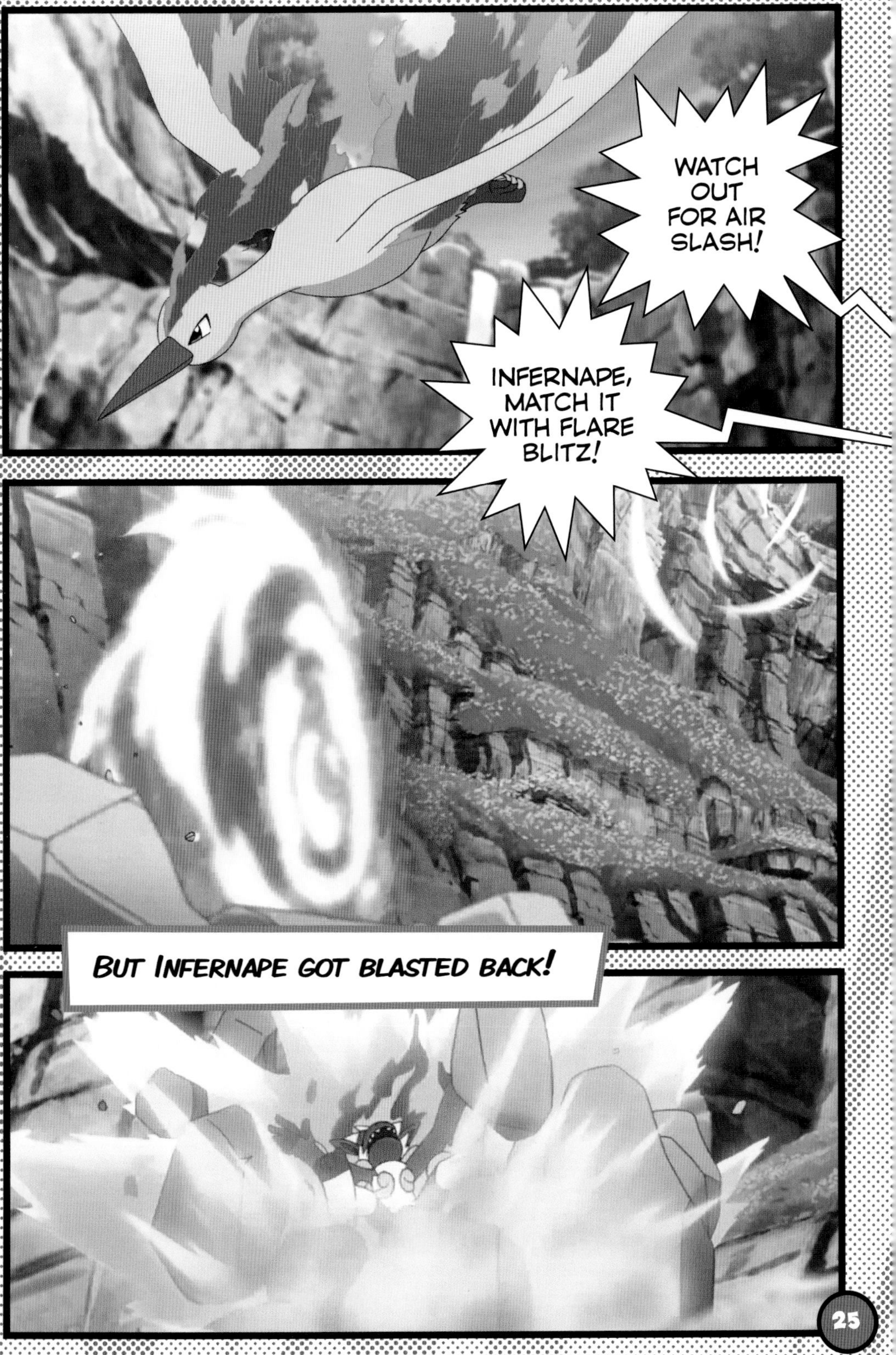
WATCH OUT FOR AIR SLASH!
INFERNAPE, MATCH IT WITH FLARE BLITZ!
BUT INFERNAPE GOT BLASTED BACK!

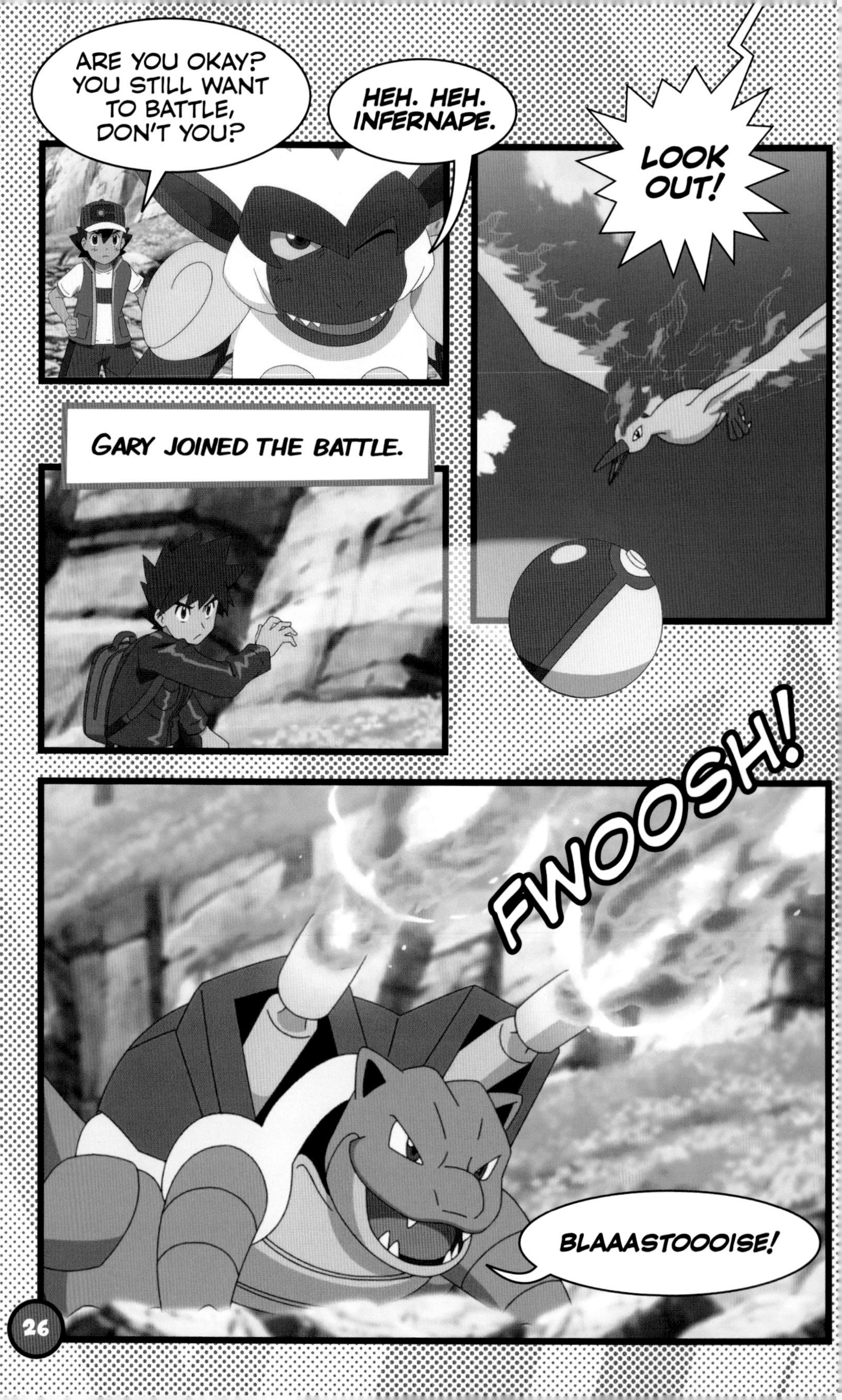
ARE YOU OKAY? YOU STILL WANT TO BATTLE, DON'T YOU?
HEH. HEH. INFERNAPE.
LOOK OUT!
GARY JOINED THE BATTLE.
FWOOSH!
BLAAASTOOOISE!

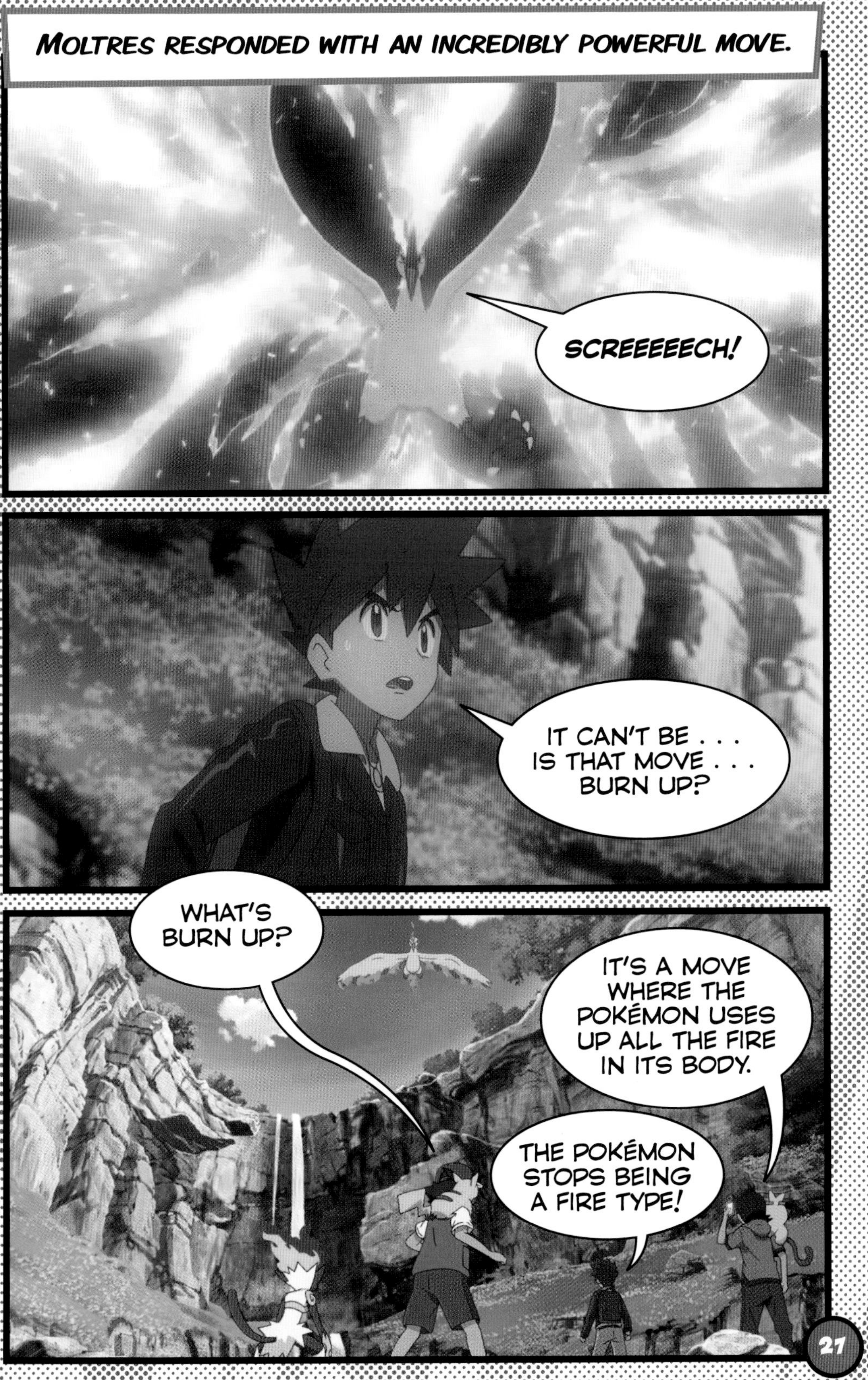
MOLTRES RESPONDED WITH AN INCREDIBLY POWERFUL MOVE.
SCREEEEECH!
IT CAN'T BE . . . IS THAT MOVE . . . BURN UP?
WHAT'S BURN UP?
IT'S A MOVE WHERE THE POKÉMON USES UP ALL THE FIRE IN ITS BODY.
THE POKÉMON STOPS BEING A FIRE TYPE!

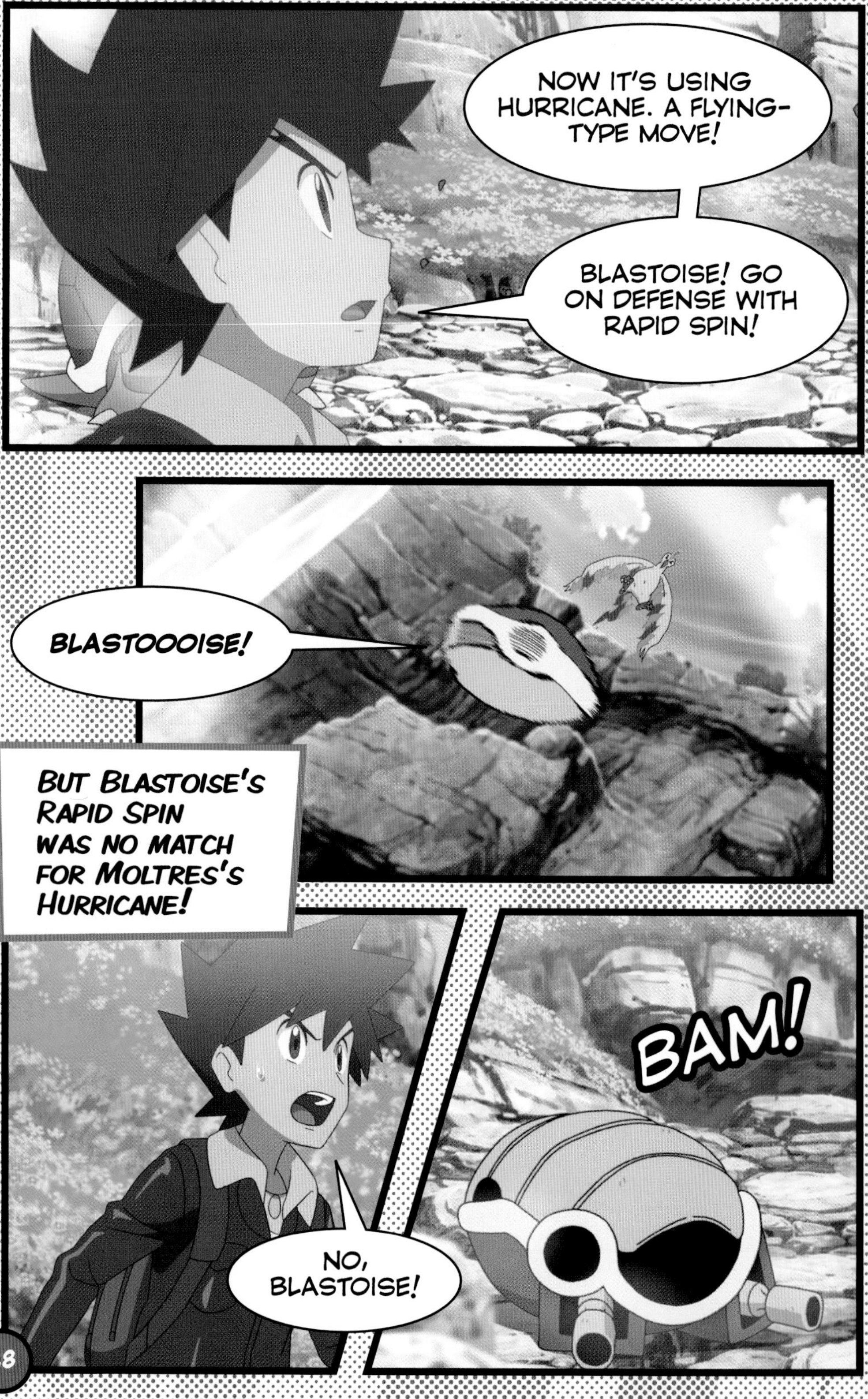
NOW IT'S USING HURRICANE. A FLYING-TYPE MOVE!
BLASTOISE! GO ON DEFENSE WITH RAPID SPIN!
BLASTOOOISE!
BUT BLASTOISE'S RAPID SPIN WAS NO MATCH FOR MOLTRES'S HURRICANE!
NO, BLASTOISE!
BAM!

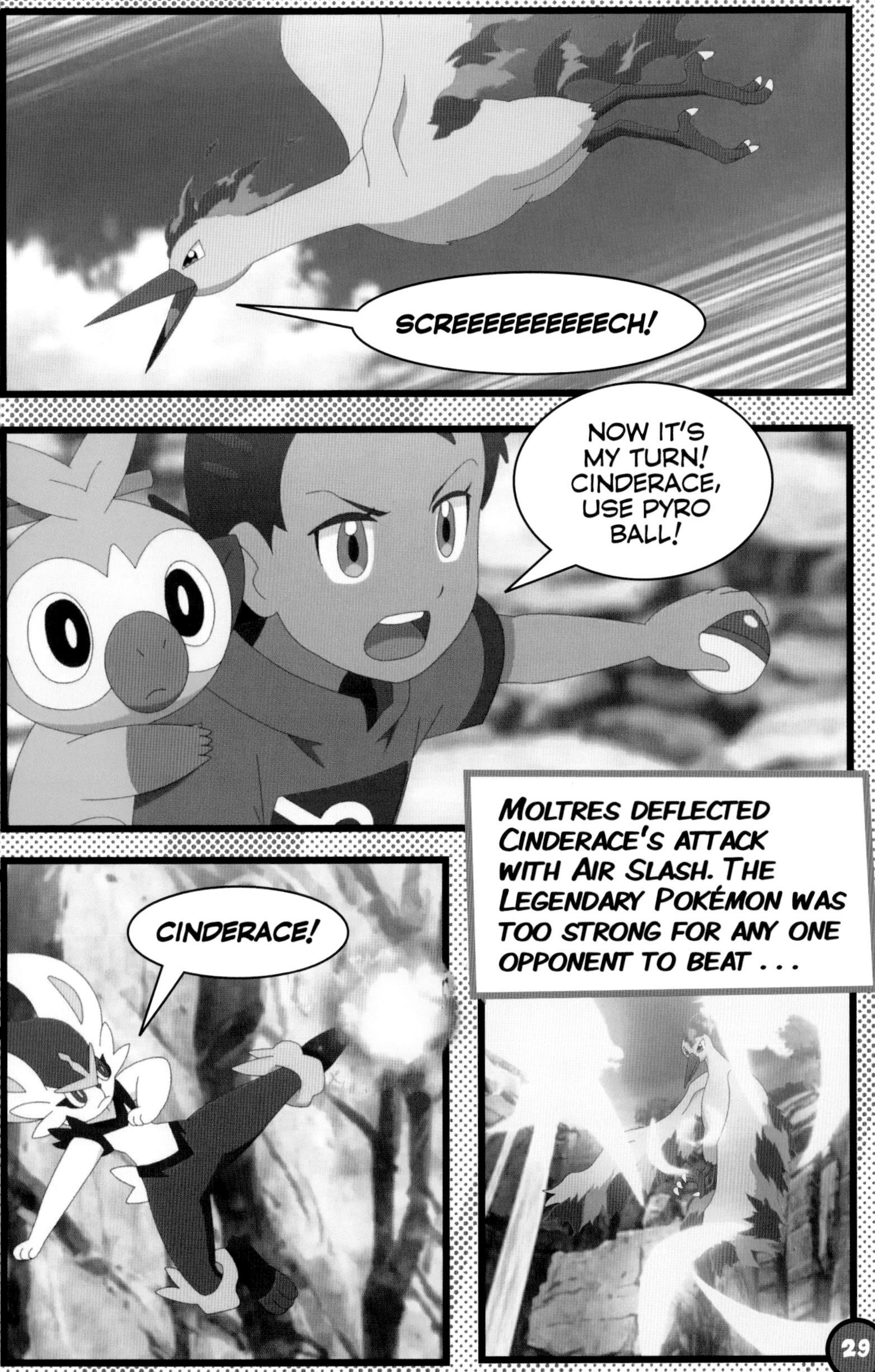
SCREEEEEEEEEEECH!
NOW IT'S MY TURN! CINDERACE, USE PYRO BALL!
MOLTRES DEFLECTED CINDERACE'S ATTACK WITH AIR SLASH. THE LEGENDARY POKÉMON WAS TOO STRONG FOR ANY ONE OPPONENT TO BEAT . . .
CINDERACE!

THE FRIENDS NEEDED TO WORK AS A TEAM!

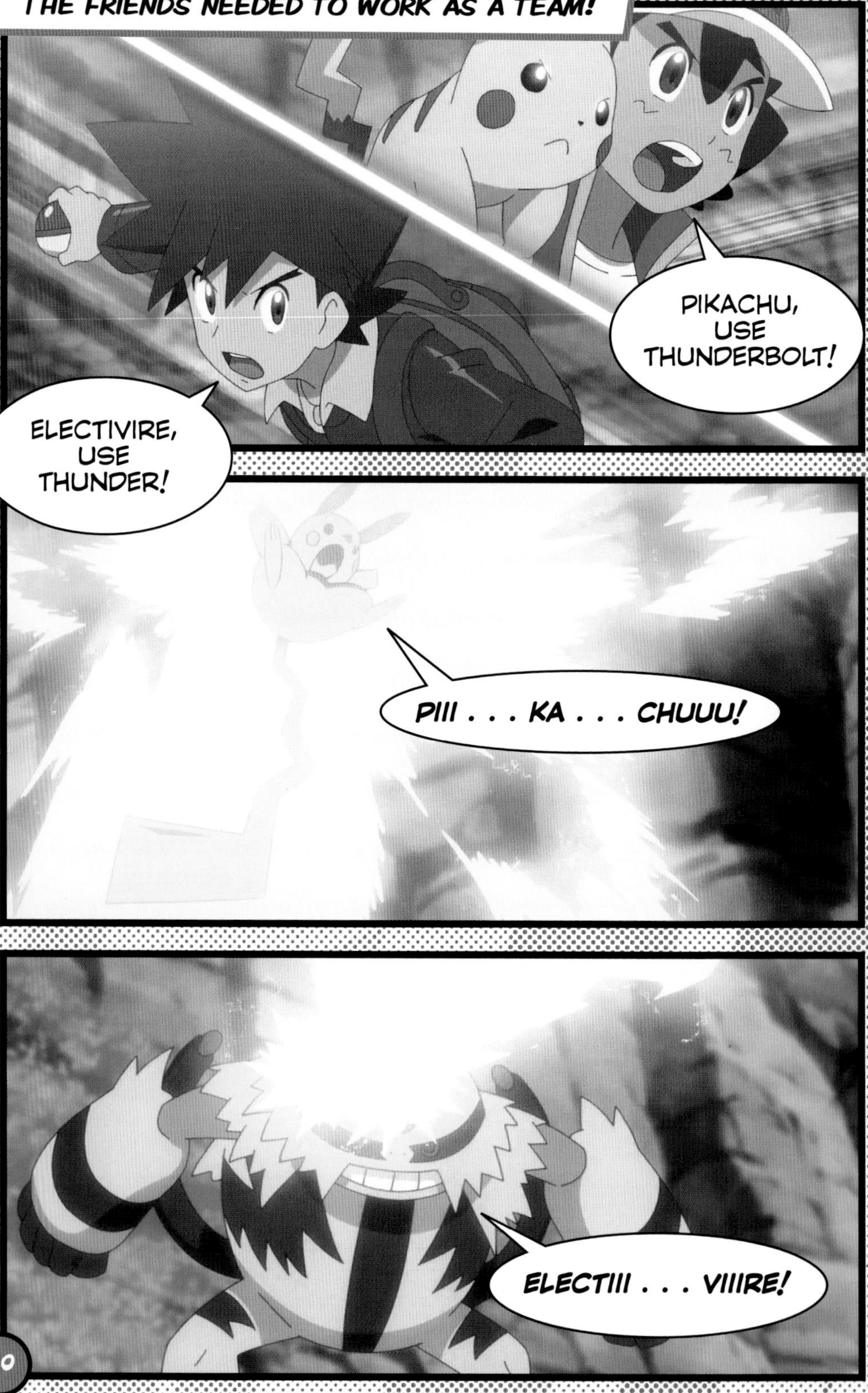
PIKACHU, USE THUNDERBOLT!
ELECTIVIRE, USE THUNDER!
PIII . . . KA . . . CHUUU!
ELECTIII . . . VIIIRE!

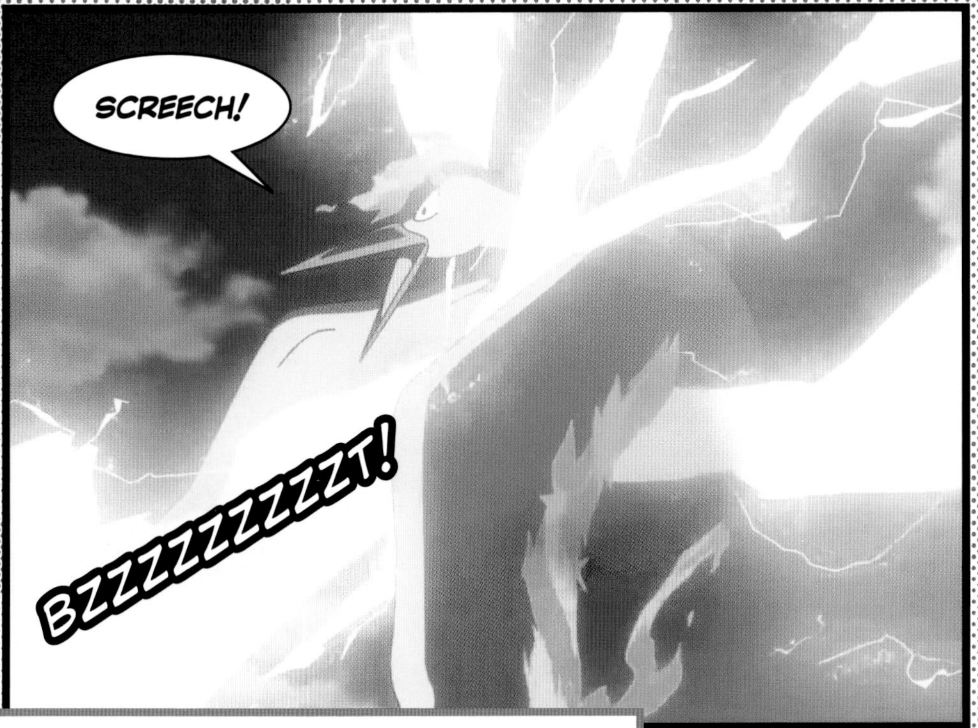
SCREECH!
BZZZZZZZZZT!

MOLTRES WAS FINALLY OVERPOWERED!

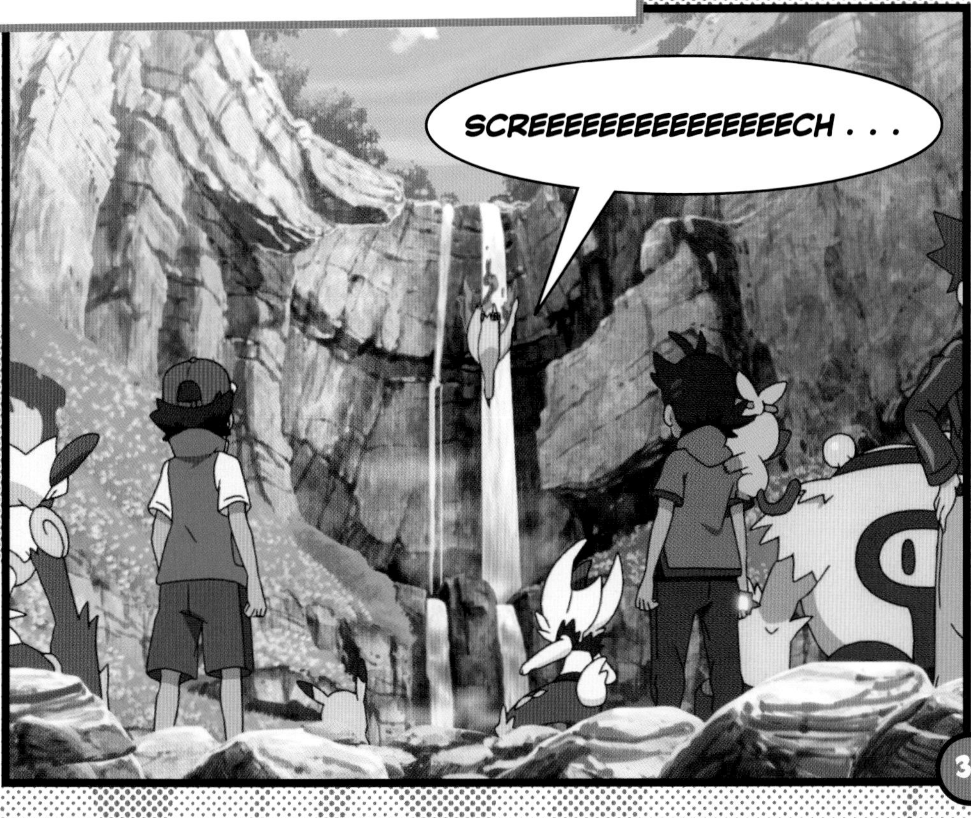
SCREEEEEEEEEEEEEEECH . . .

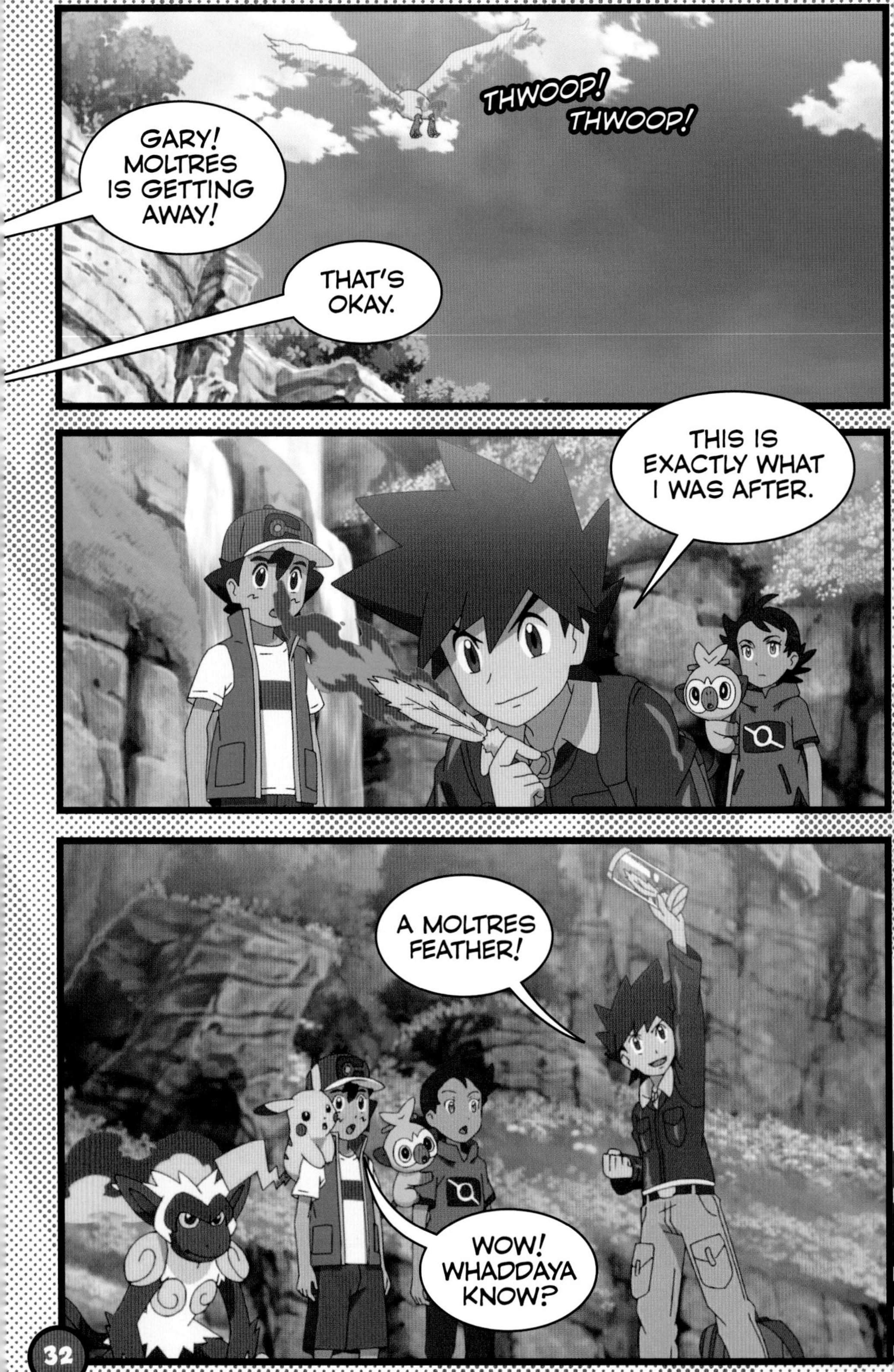
THWOOP! THWOOP!
GARY! MOLTRES IS GETTING AWAY!
THAT'S OKAY.
THIS IS EXACTLY WHAT I WAS AFTER.
A MOLTRES FEATHER!
WOW! WHADDAYA KNOW?

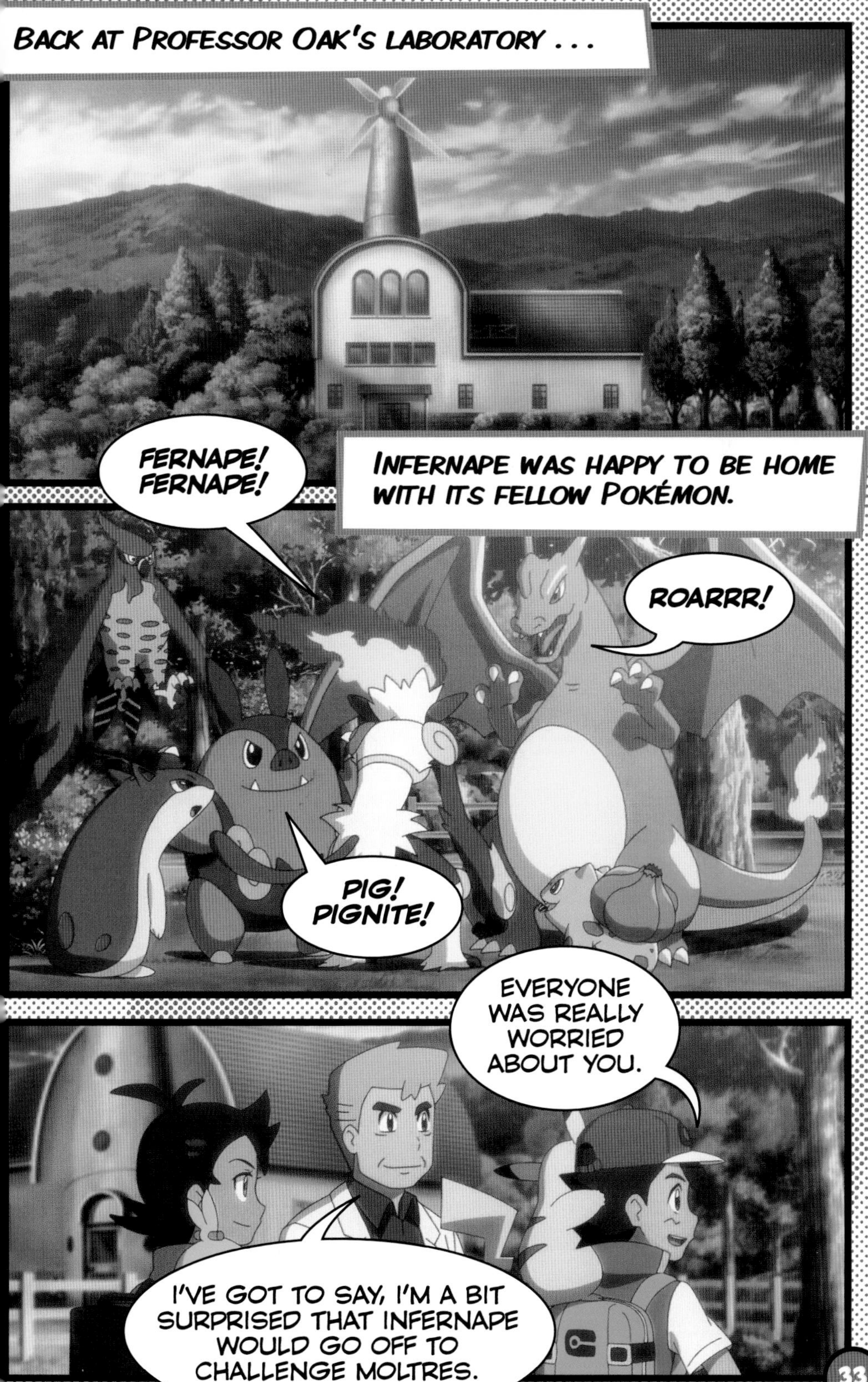
BACK AT PROFESSOR OAK'S LABORATORY . . .
INFERNAPE WAS HAPPY TO BE HOME WITH ITS FELLOW POKÉMON.
FERNAPE! FERNAPE!
ROARRR!
PIG! PIGNITE!
EVERYONE WAS REALLY WORRIED ABOUT YOU.
I'VE GOT TO SAY, I'M A BIT SURPRISED THAT INFERNAPE WOULD GO OFF TO CHALLENGE MOLTRES.

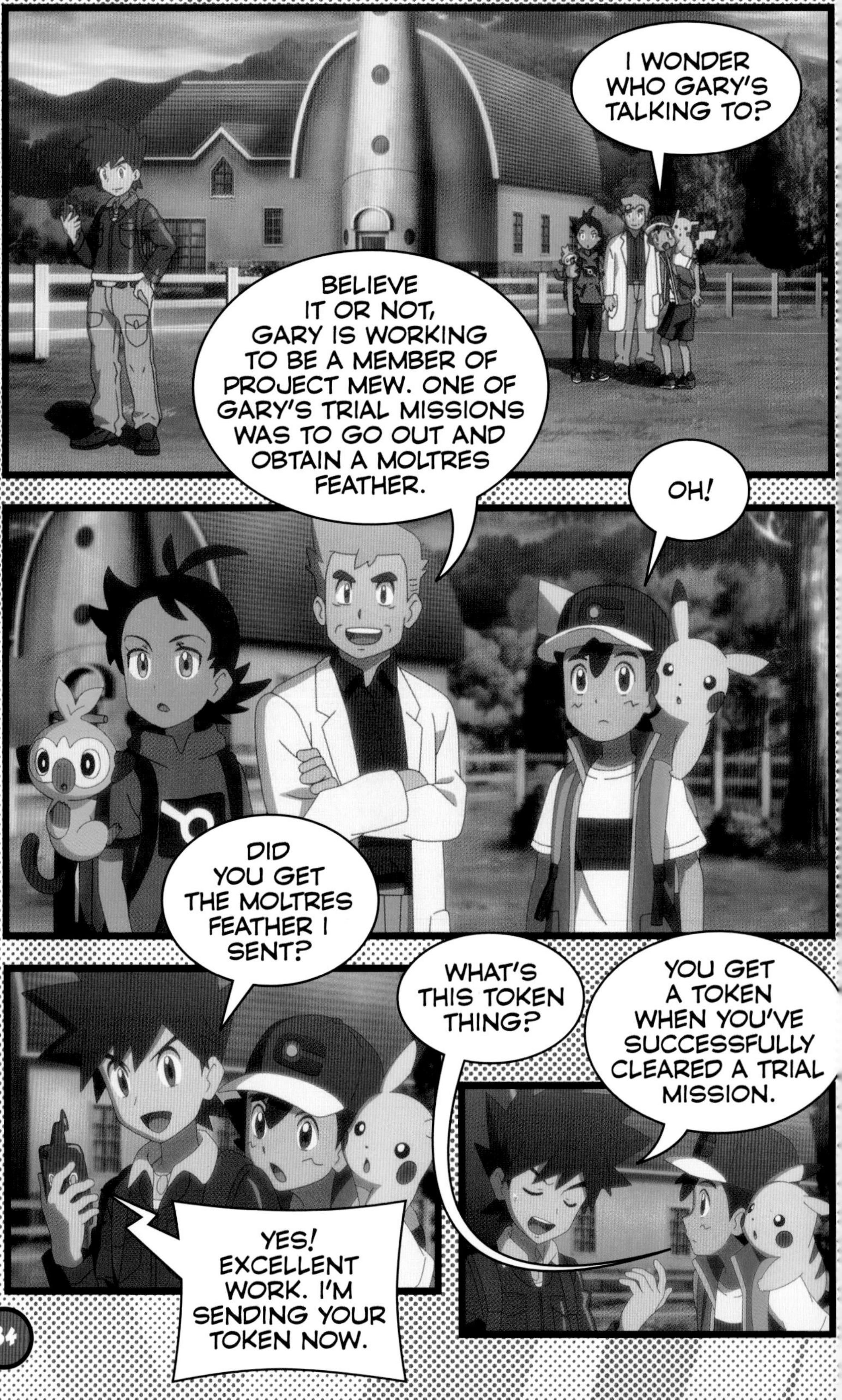
I WONDER WHO GARY'S TALKING TO?
BELIEVE IT OR NOT, GARY IS WORKING TO BE A MEMBER OF PROJECT MEW. ONE OF GARY'S TRIAL MISSIONS WAS TO GO OUT AND OBTAIN A MOLTRES FEATHER.
OH!
DID YOU GET THE MOLTRES FEATHER I SENT?
YES! EXCELLENT WORK. I'M SENDING YOUR TOKEN NOW.
WHAT'S THIS TOKEN THING?
YOU GET A TOKEN WHEN YOU'VE SUCCESSFULLY CLEARED A TRIAL MISSION.

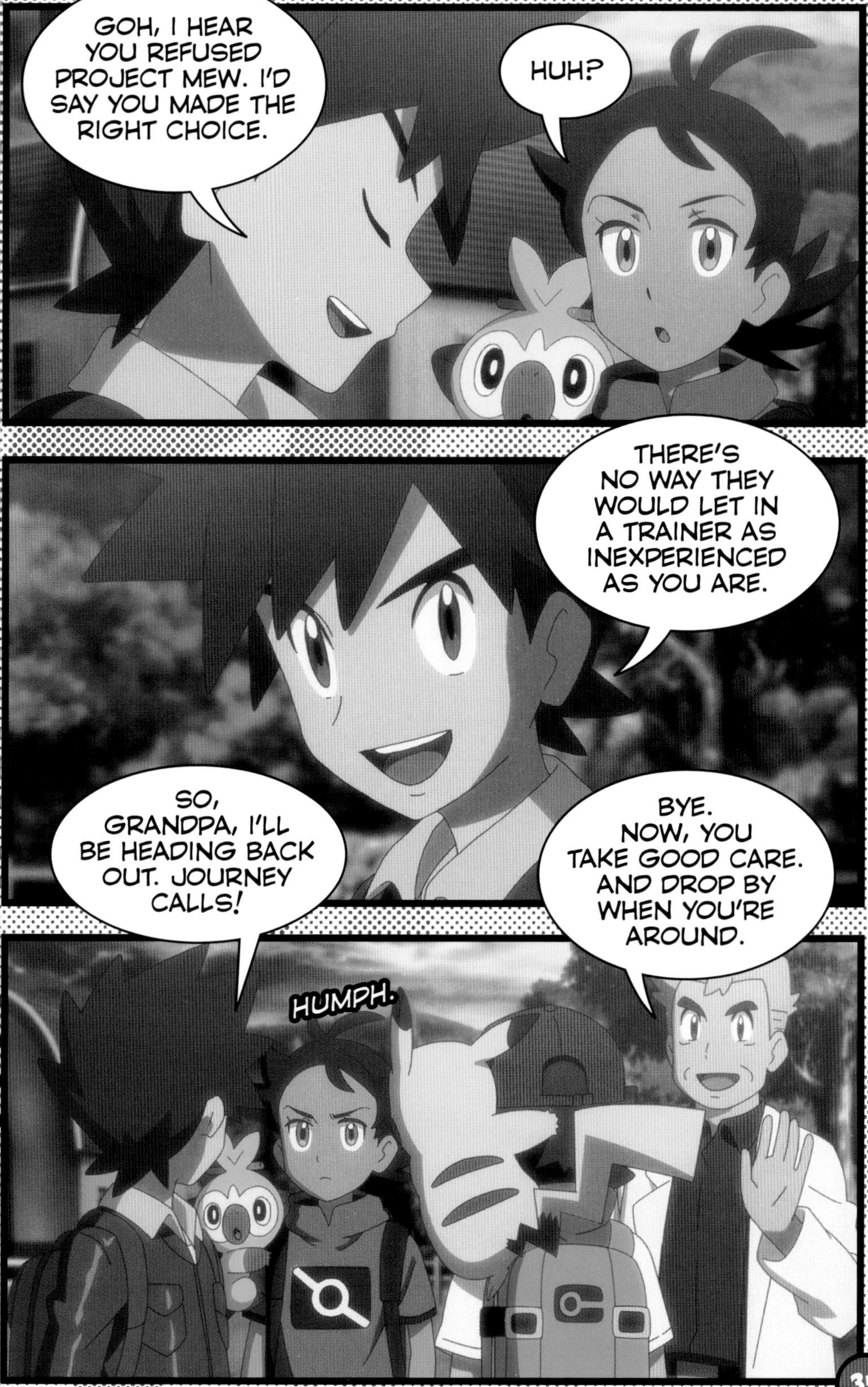
GOH, I HEAR YOU REFUSED PROJECT MEW. I'D SAY YOU MADE THE RIGHT CHOICE.
HUH?
THERE'S NO WAY THEY WOULD LET IN A TRAINER AS INEXPERIENCED AS YOU ARE.
SO, GRANDPA, I'LL BE HEADING BACK OUT. JOURNEY CALLS!
BYE. NOW, YOU TAKE GOOD CARE. AND DROP BY WHEN YOU'RE AROUND.
HUMPH.

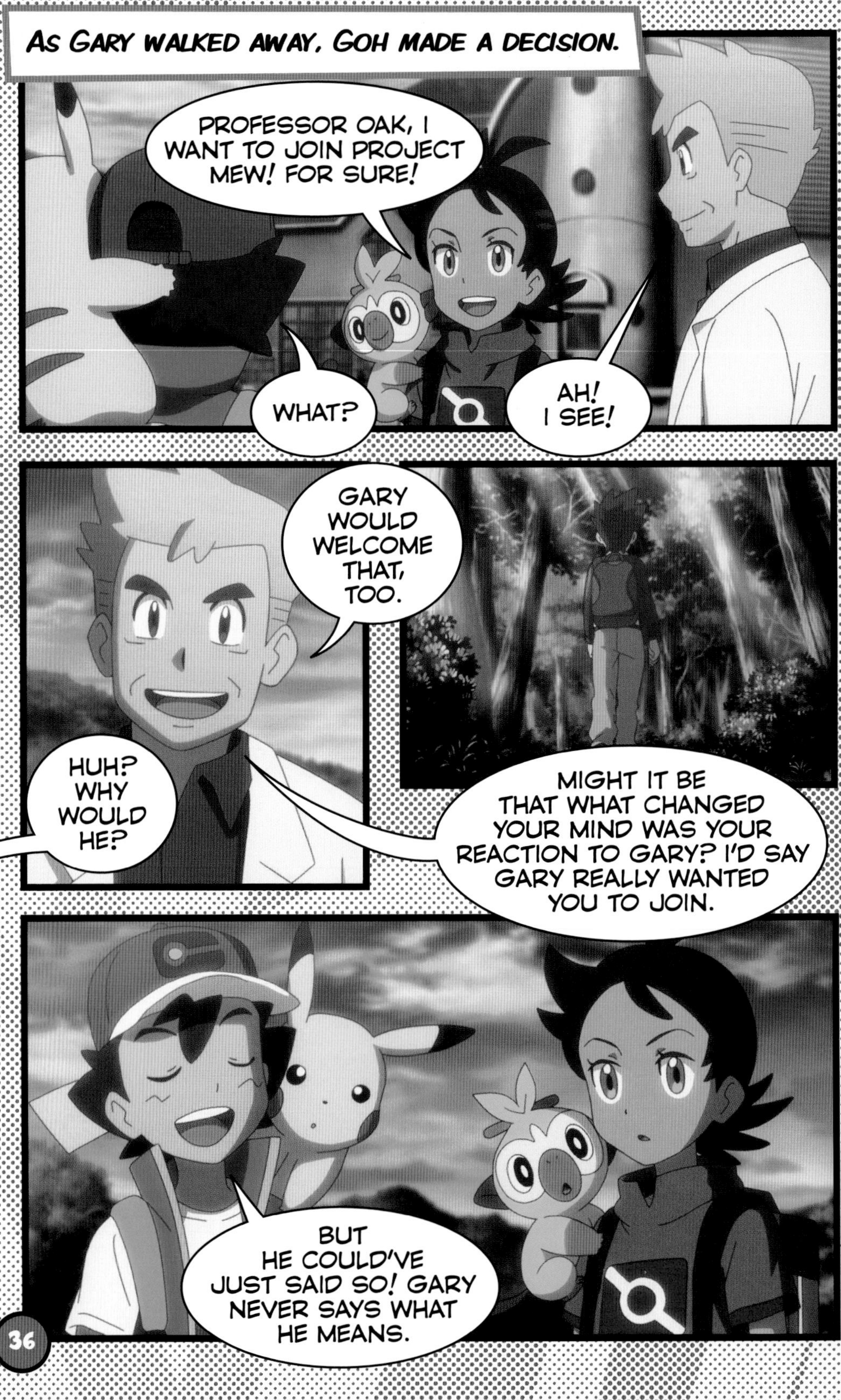

As Gary walked away, Goh made a decision.
PROFESSOR OAK, I WANT TO JOIN PROJECT MEW! FOR SURE!
WHAT?
AH! I SEE!
GARY WOULD WELCOME THAT, TOO.
HUH? WHY WOULD HE?
MIGHT IT BE THAT WHAT CHANGED YOUR MIND WAS YOUR REACTION TO GARY? I'D SAY GARY REALLY WANTED YOU TO JOIN.
BUT HE COULD'VE JUST SAID SO! GARY NEVER SAYS WHAT HE MEANS.

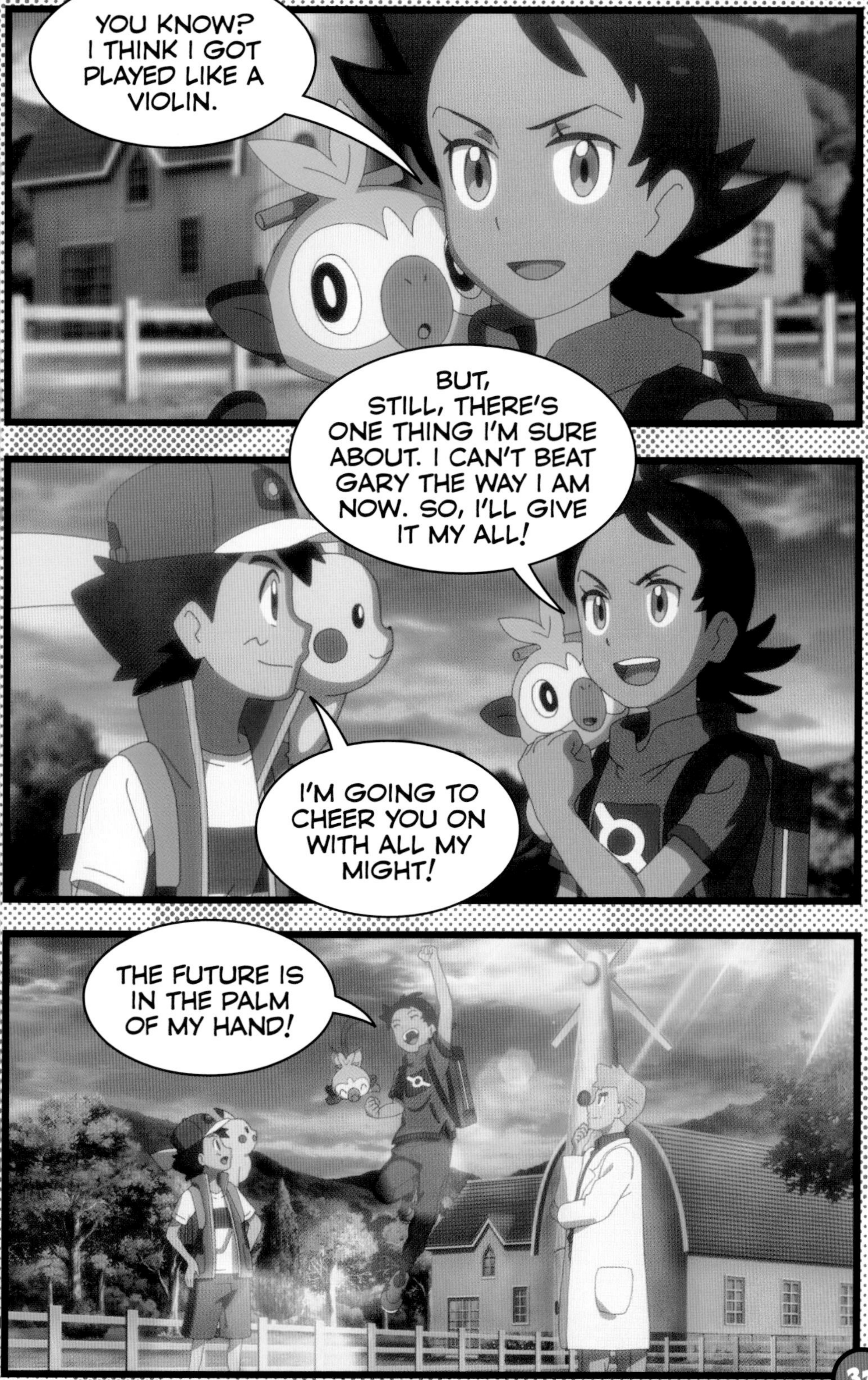
YOU KNOW? I THINK I GOT PLAYED LIKE A VIOLIN.
BUT, STILL, THERE'S ONE THING I'M SURE ABOUT. I CAN'T BEAT GARY THE WAY I AM NOW. SO, I'LL GIVE IT MY ALL!
I'M GOING TO CHEER YOU ON WITH ALL MY MIGHT!
THE FUTURE IS IN THE PALM OF MY HAND!

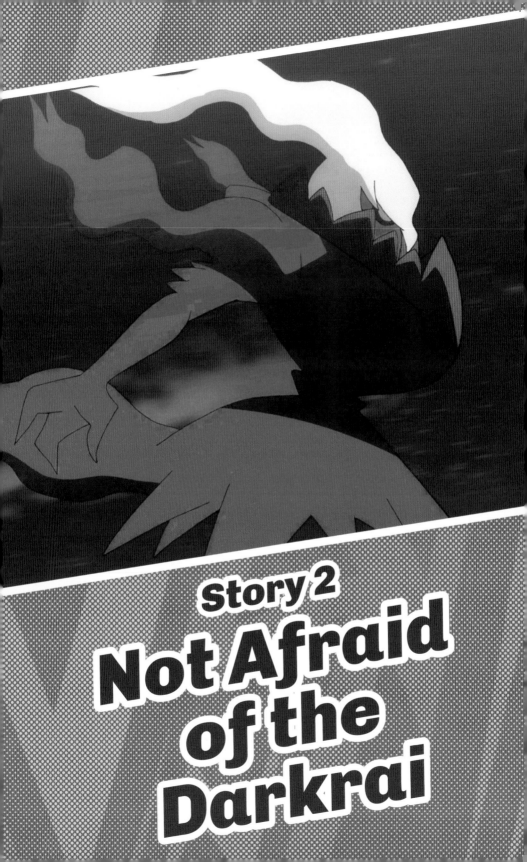

Story 2

Not Afraid of the Darkrai

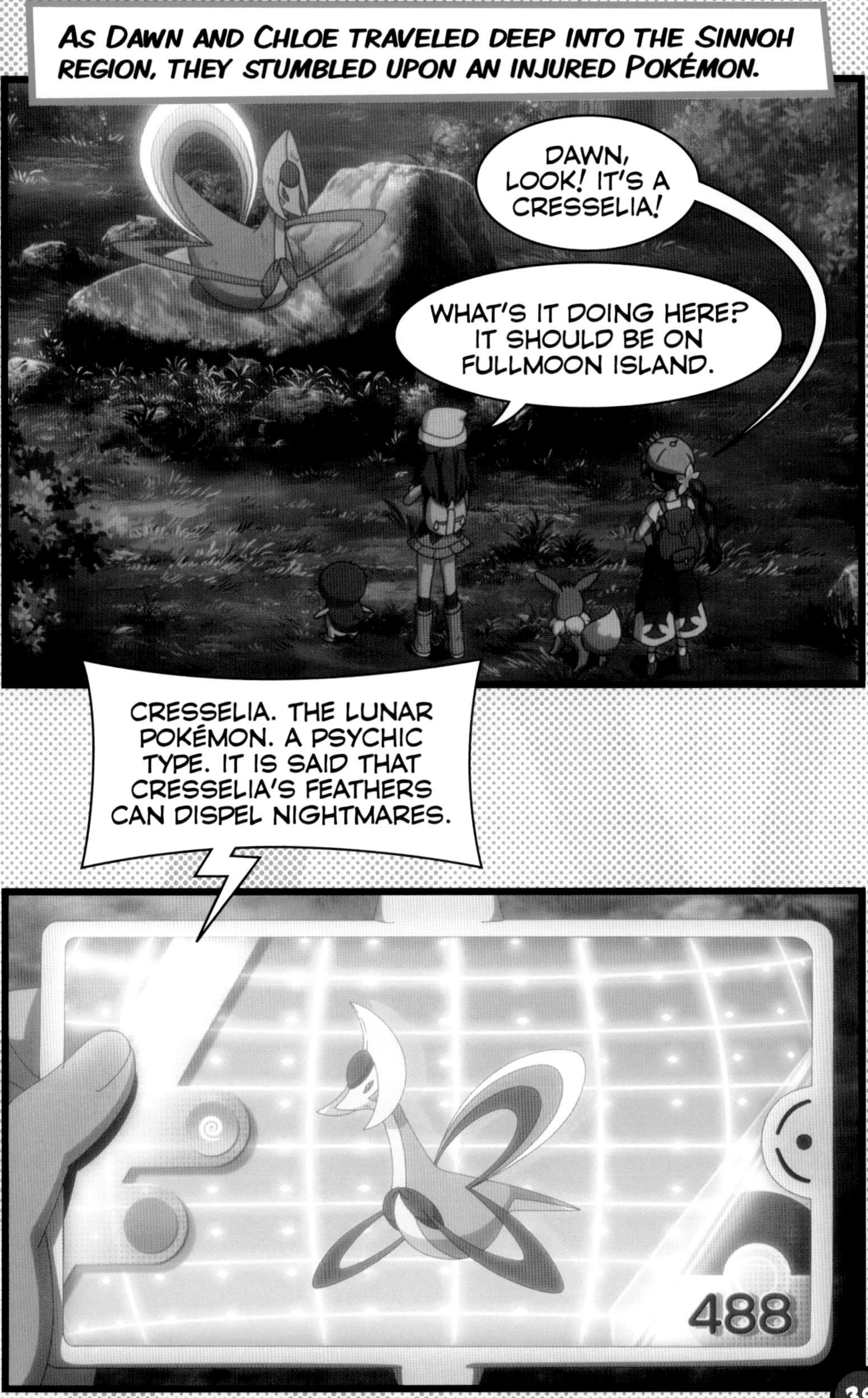
AS DAWN AND CHLOE TRAVELED DEEP INTO THE SINNOH REGION, THEY STUMBLED UPON AN INJURED POKÉMON.
DAWN, LOOK! IT'S A CRESSELIA!
WHAT'S IT DOING HERE? IT SHOULD BE ON FULLMOON ISLAND.
CRESSELIA. THE LUNAR POKÉMON. A PSYCHIC TYPE. IT IS SAID THAT CRESSELIA'S FEATHERS CAN DISPEL NIGHTMARES.
488

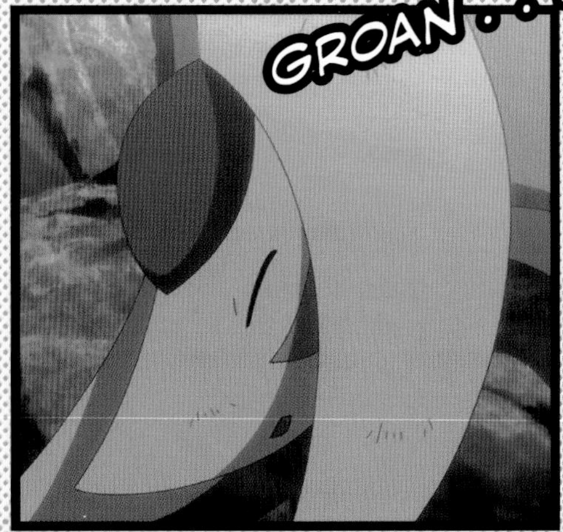
GROAN . . .

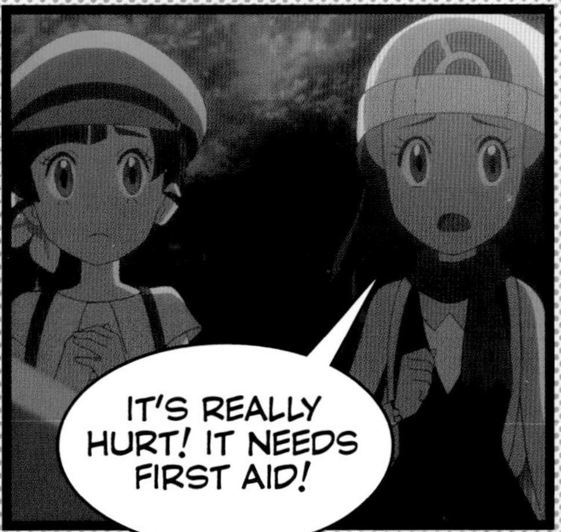
IT'S REALLY HURT! IT NEEDS FIRST AID!

BUT CRESSELIA DIDN'T TRUST THEM.

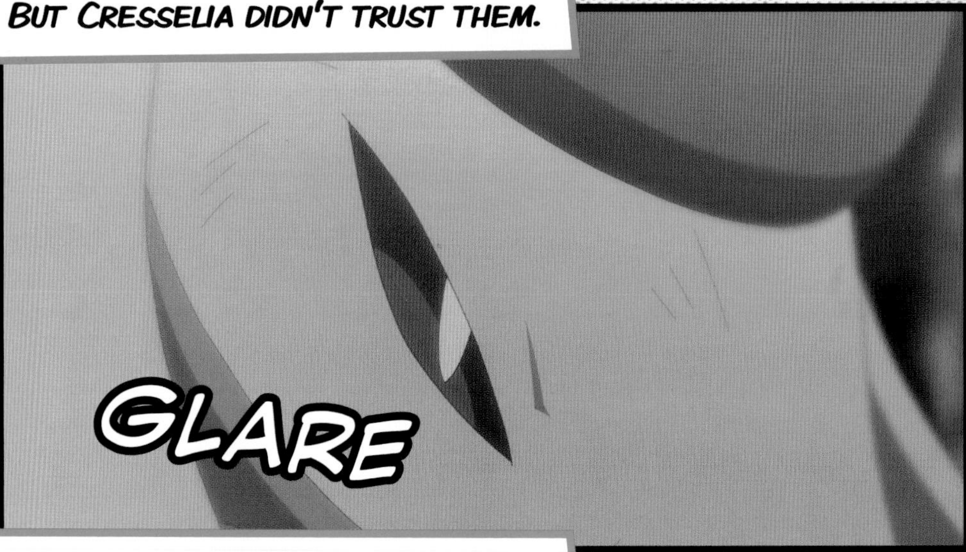
GLARE

IT SENT A PSYCHO CUT THEIR WAY.

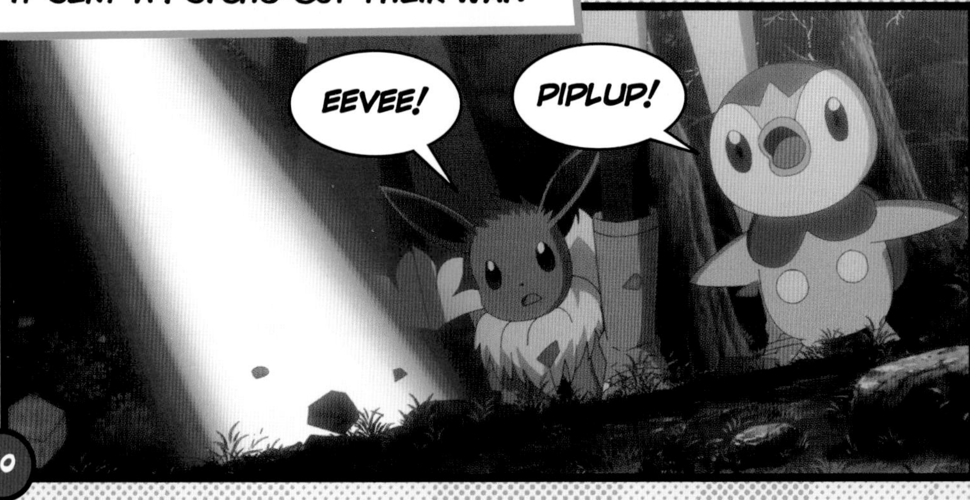
EEVEE!
PIPLUP!

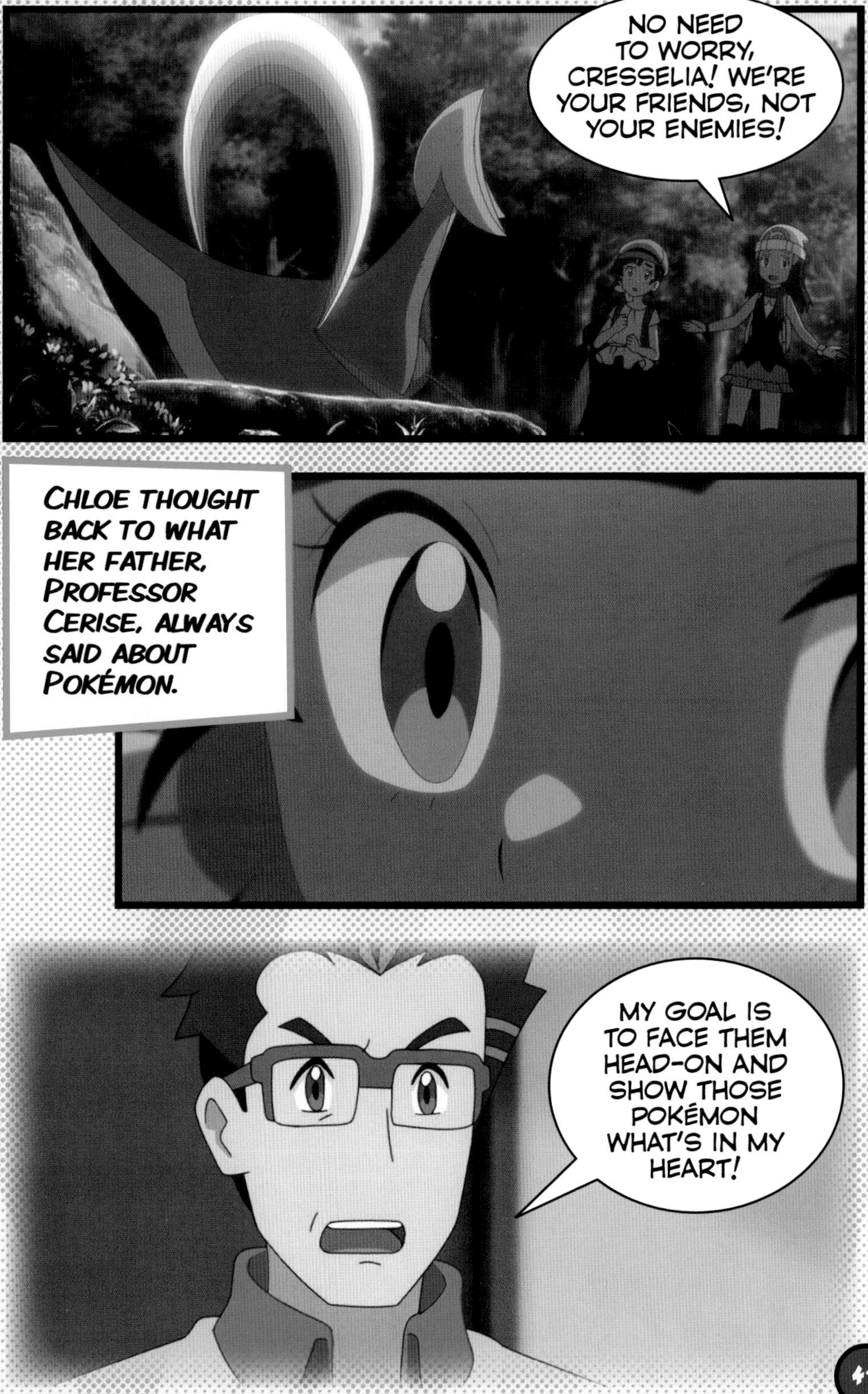
NO NEED TO WORRY, CRESSELIA! WE'RE YOUR FRIENDS, NOT YOUR ENEMIES!
CHLOE THOUGHT BACK TO WHAT HER FATHER, PROFESSOR CERISE, ALWAYS SAID ABOUT POKÉMON.
MY GOAL IS TO FACE THEM HEAD-ON AND SHOW THOSE POKÉMON WHAT'S IN MY HEART!

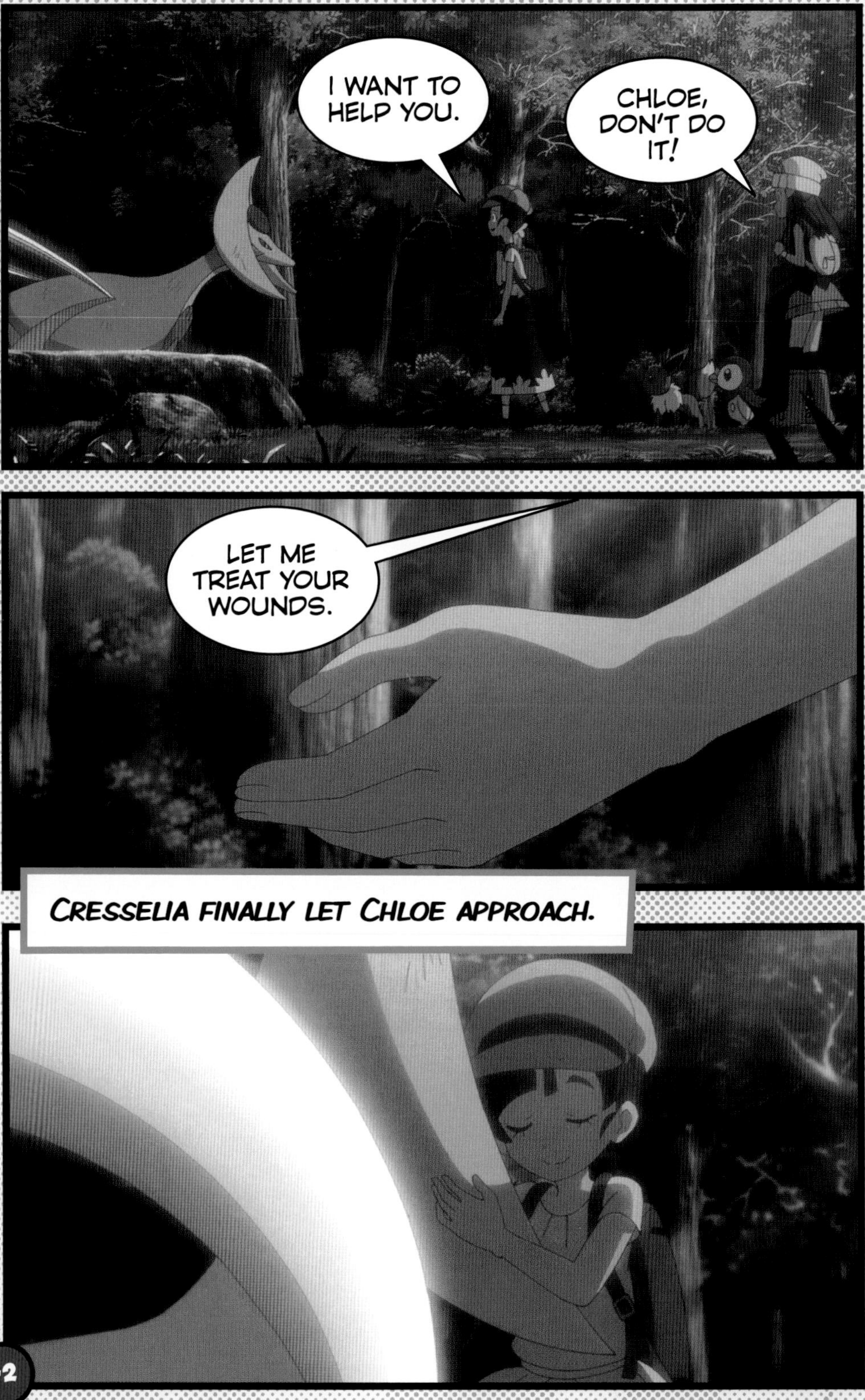
I WANT TO HELP YOU.
CHLOE, DON'T DO IT!
LET ME TREAT YOUR WOUNDS.
CRESSELIA FINALLY LET CHLOE APPROACH.

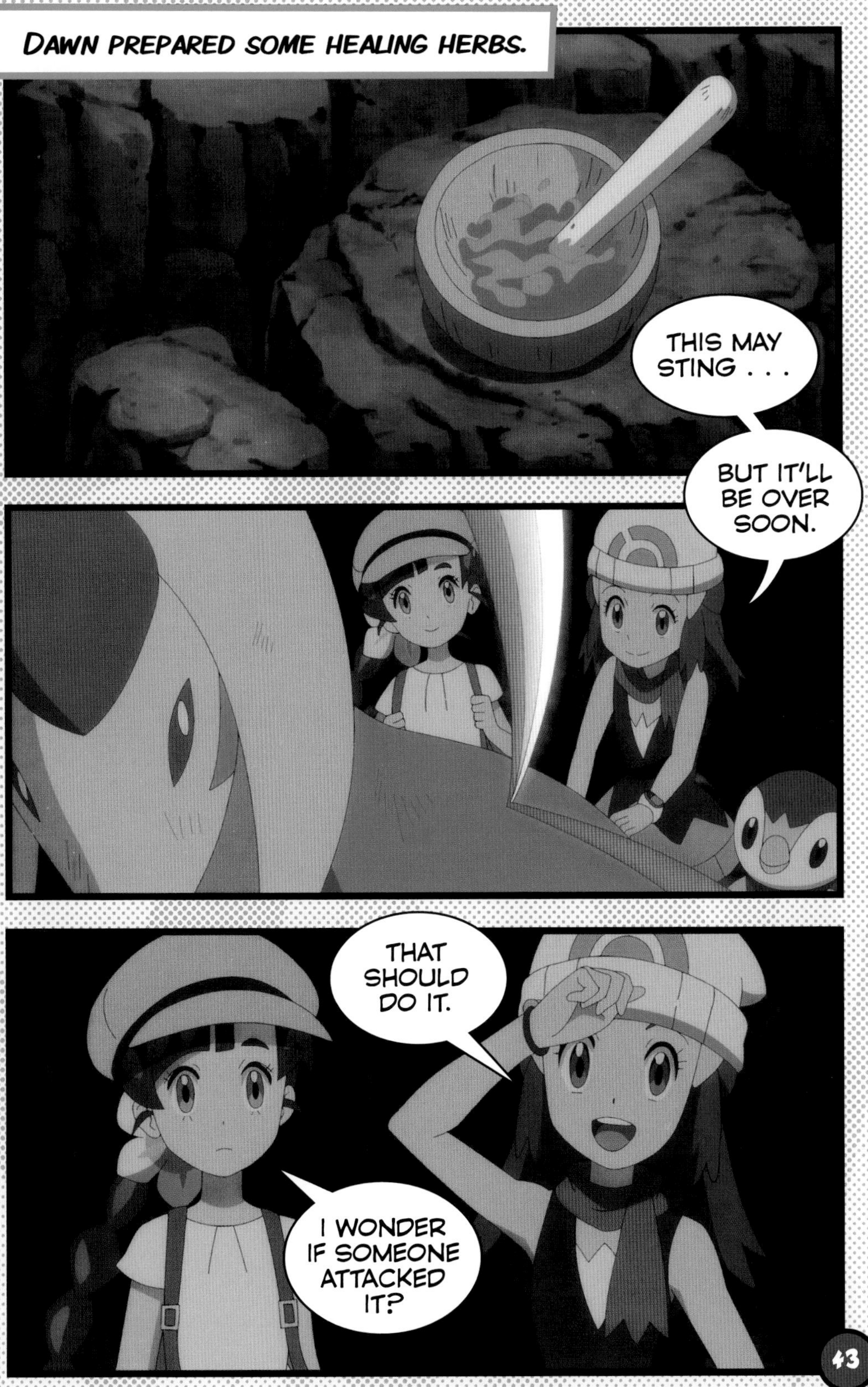
DAWN PREPARED SOME HEALING HERBS.
THIS MAY STING . . .
BUT IT'LL BE OVER SOON.
THAT SHOULD DO IT.
I WONDER IF SOMEONE ATTACKED IT?

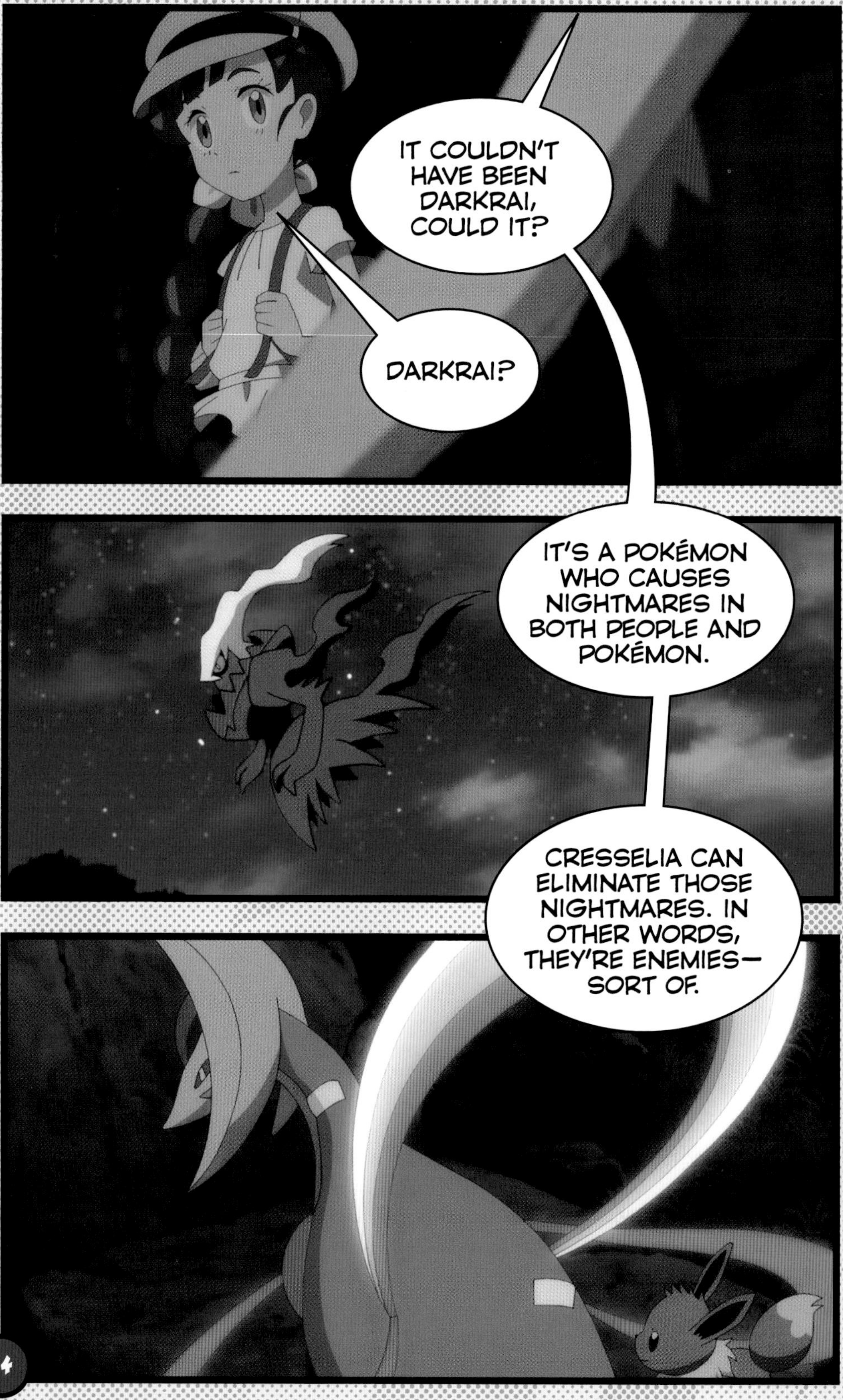
IT COULDN'T HAVE BEEN DARKRAI, COULD IT?
DARKRAI?
IT'S A POKÉMON WHO CAUSES NIGHTMARES IN BOTH PEOPLE AND POKÉMON.
CRESSELIA CAN ELIMINATE THOSE NIGHTMARES. IN OTHER WORDS, THEY'RE ENEMIES—SORT OF.

AFTER HELPING CRESSELIA, DAWN AND CHLOE SET UP CAMP FOR THE NIGHT.

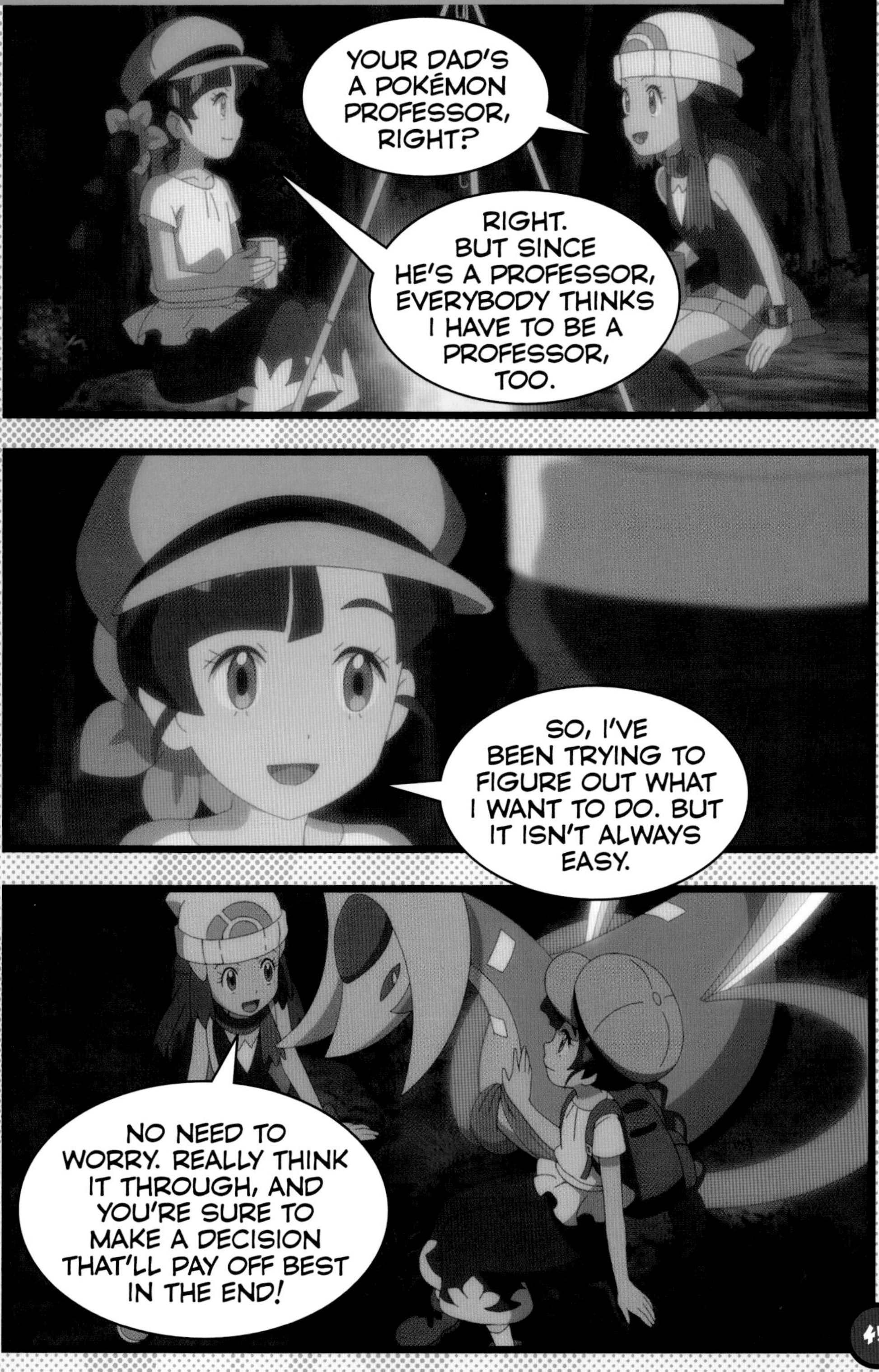
YOUR DAD'S A POKÉMON PROFESSOR, RIGHT?
RIGHT. BUT SINCE HE'S A PROFESSOR, EVERYBODY THINKS I HAVE TO BE A PROFESSOR, TOO.
SO, I'VE BEEN TRYING TO FIGURE OUT WHAT I WANT TO DO. BUT IT ISN'T ALWAYS EASY.
NO NEED TO WORRY. REALLY THINK IT THROUGH, AND YOU'RE SURE TO MAKE A DECISION THAT'LL PAY OFF BEST IN THE END!

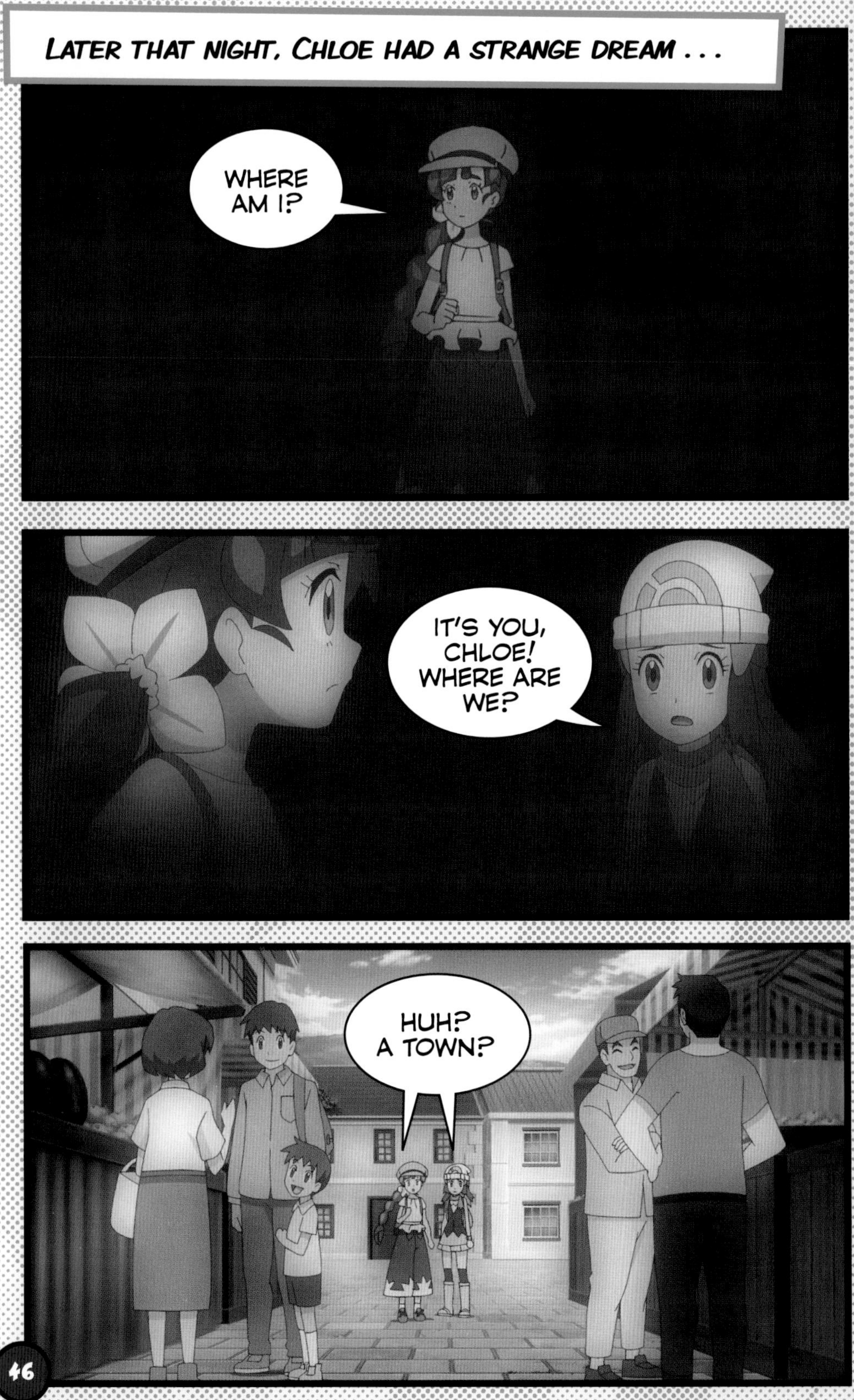
LATER THAT NIGHT, CHLOE HAD A STRANGE DREAM . . .
WHERE AM I?
IT'S YOU, CHLOE! WHERE ARE WE?
HUH? A TOWN?

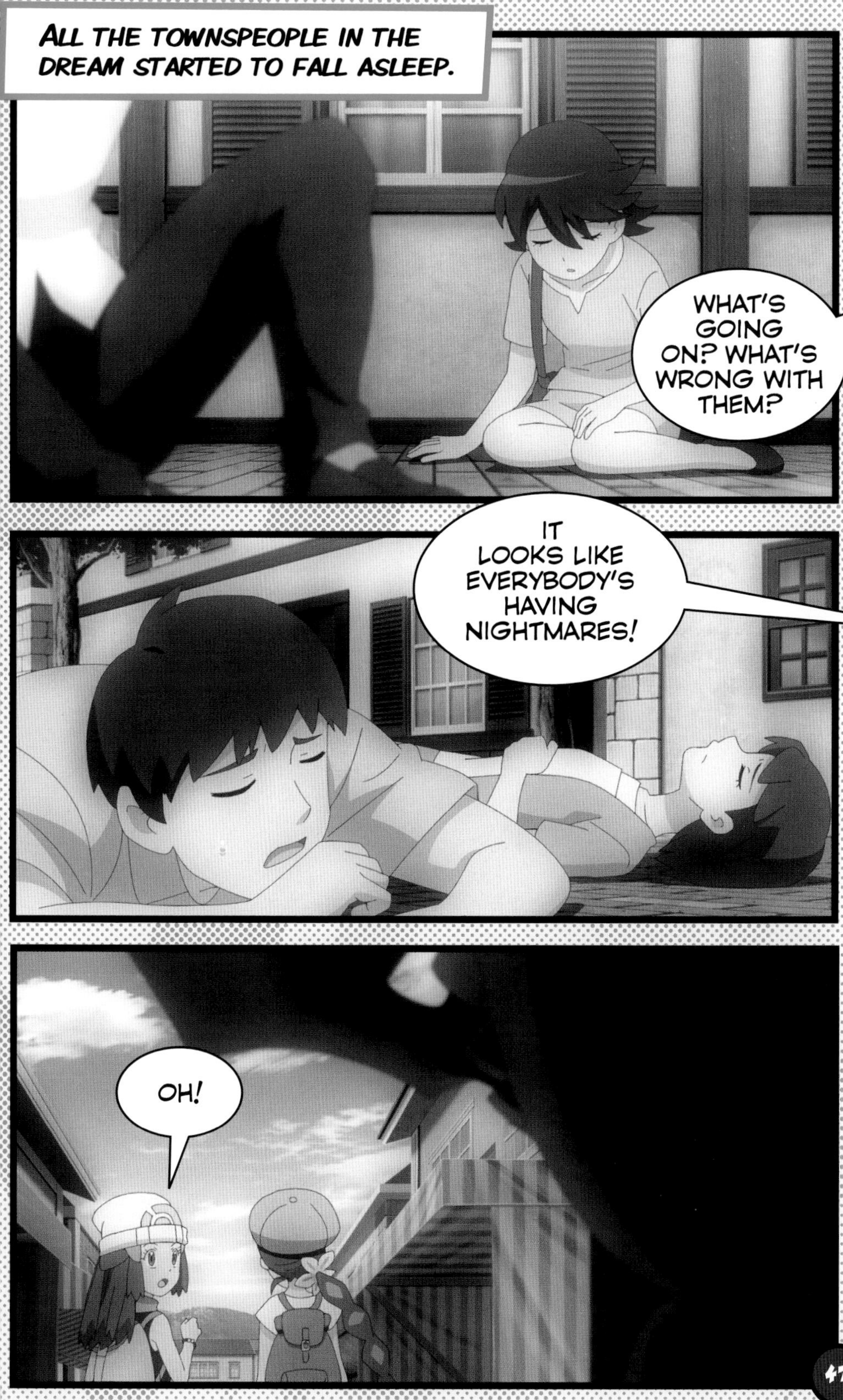
ALL THE TOWNSPEOPLE IN THE DREAM STARTED TO FALL ASLEEP.
WHAT'S GOING ON? WHAT'S WRONG WITH THEM?
IT LOOKS LIKE EVERYBODY'S HAVING NIGHTMARES!
OH!

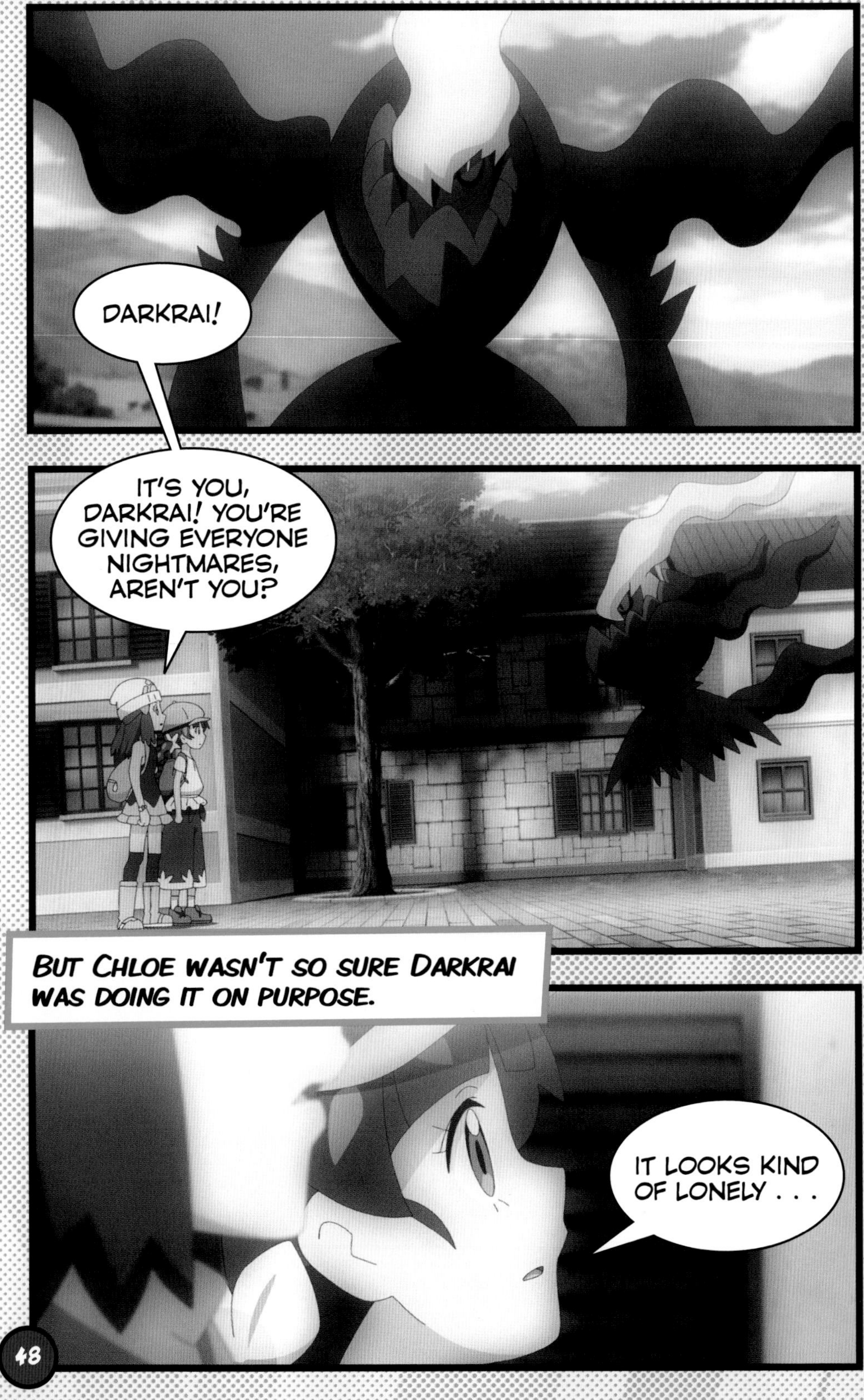
DARKRAI!
IT'S YOU, DARKRAI! YOU'RE GIVING EVERYONE NIGHTMARES, AREN'T YOU?
BUT CHLOE WASN'T SO SURE DARKRAI WAS DOING IT ON PURPOSE.
IT LOOKS KIND OF LONELY . . .

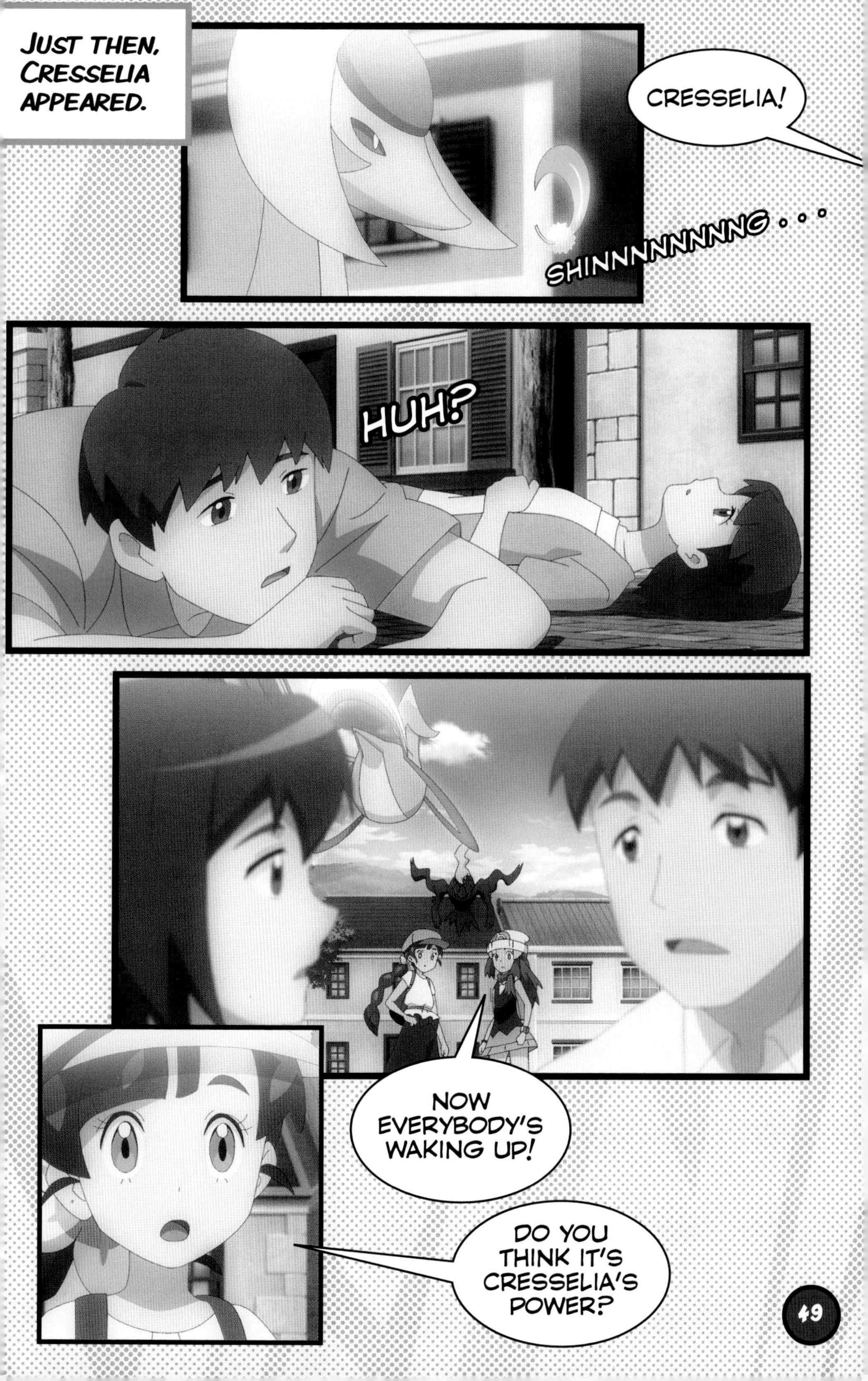

JUST THEN, CRESSELIA APPEARED.
CRESSELIA!
SHINNNNNNNNG . . .
HUH?
NOW EVERYBODY'S WAKING UP!
DO YOU THINK IT'S CRESSELIA'S POWER?

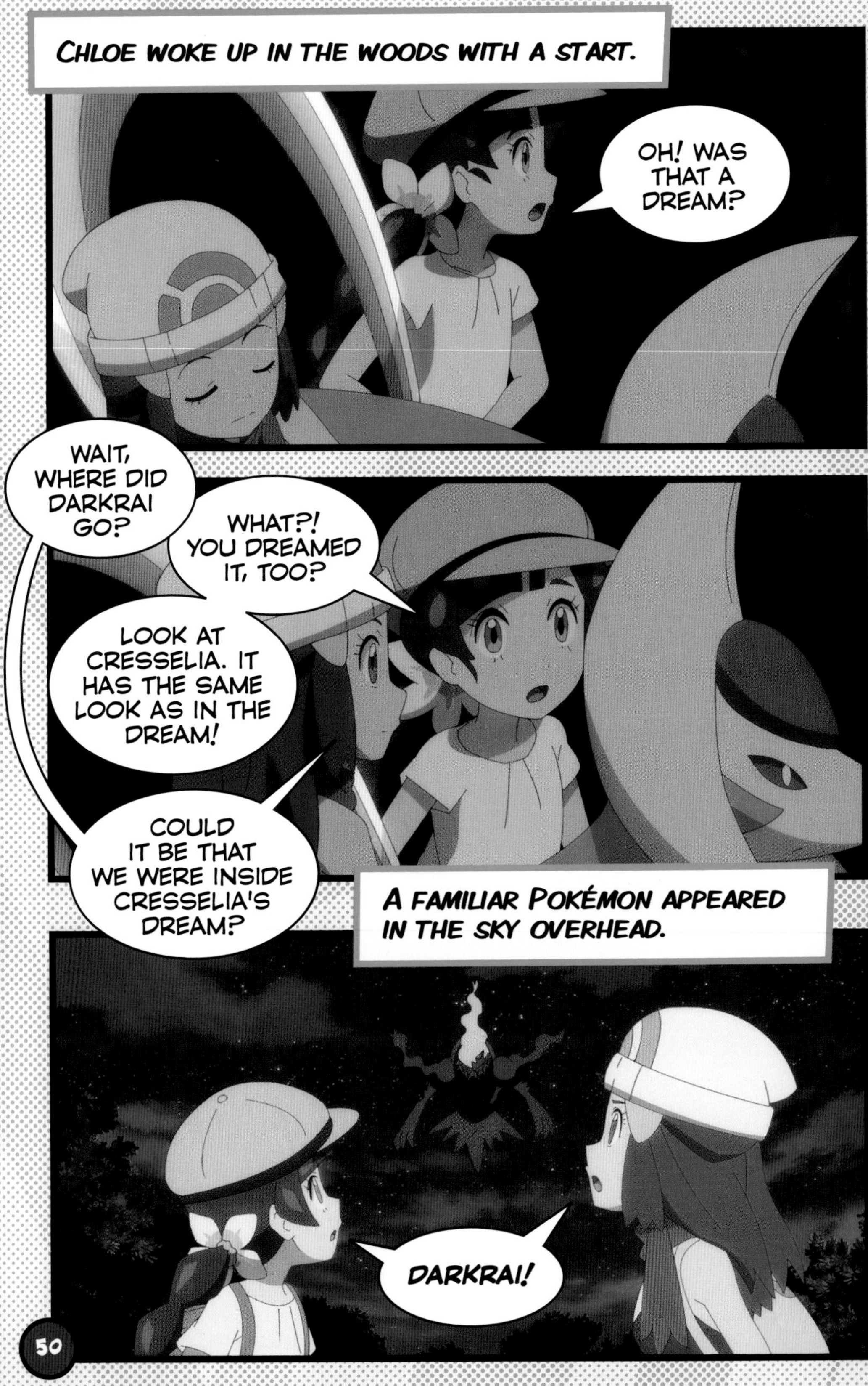
CHLOE WOKE UP IN THE WOODS WITH A START.
OH! WAS THAT A DREAM?
WAIT, WHERE DID DARKRAI GO?
WHAT?! YOU DREAMED IT, TOO?
LOOK AT CRESSELIA. IT HAS THE SAME LOOK AS IN THE DREAM!
COULD IT BE THAT WE WERE INSIDE CRESSELIA'S DREAM?
A FAMILIAR POKÉMON APPEARED IN THE SKY OVERHEAD.
DARKRAI!

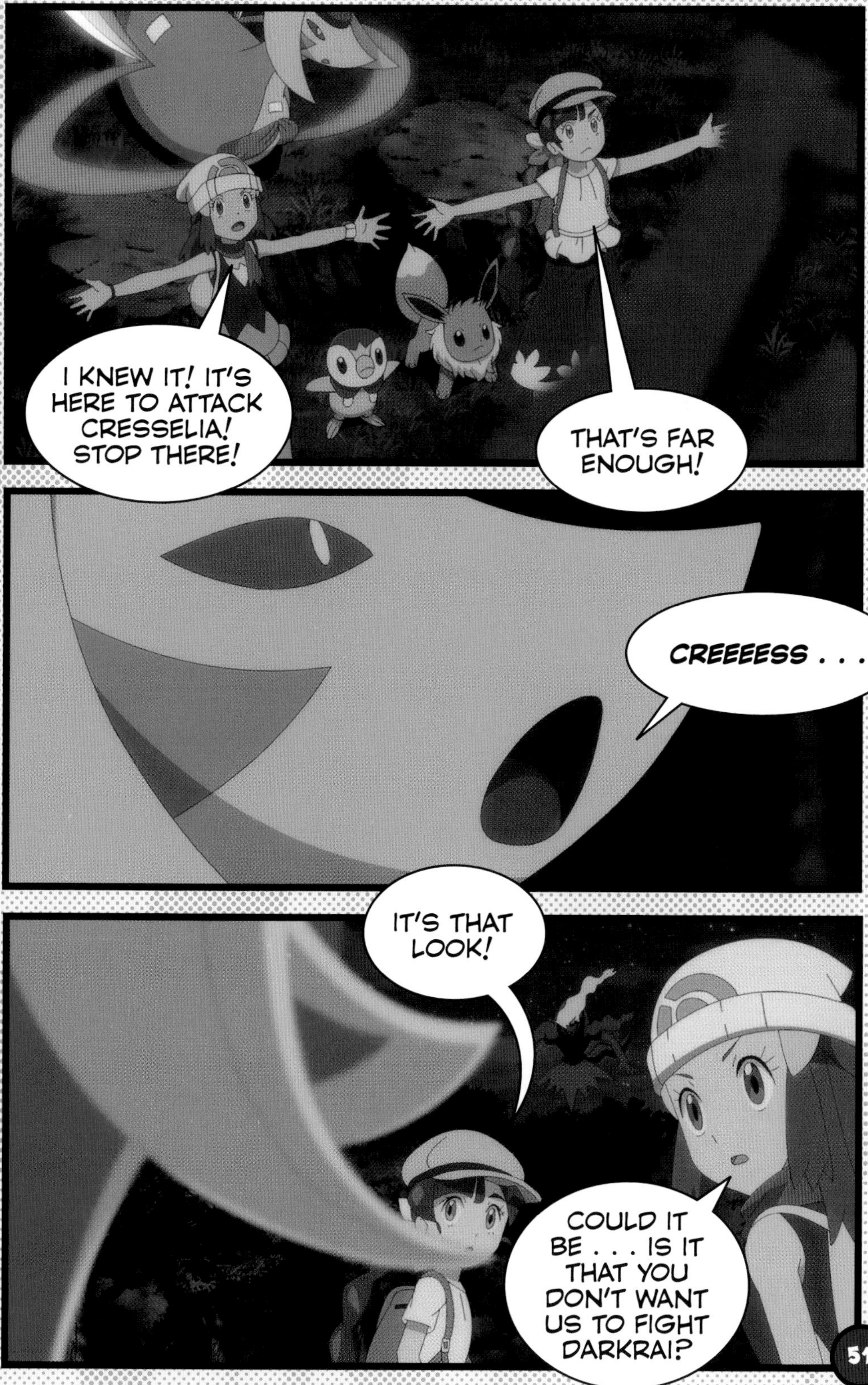
I KNEW IT! IT'S HERE TO ATTACK CRESSELIA! STOP THERE!
THAT'S FAR ENOUGH!
CREEEESS . . .
IT'S THAT LOOK!
COULD IT BE . . . IS IT THAT YOU DON'T WANT US TO FIGHT DARKRAI?

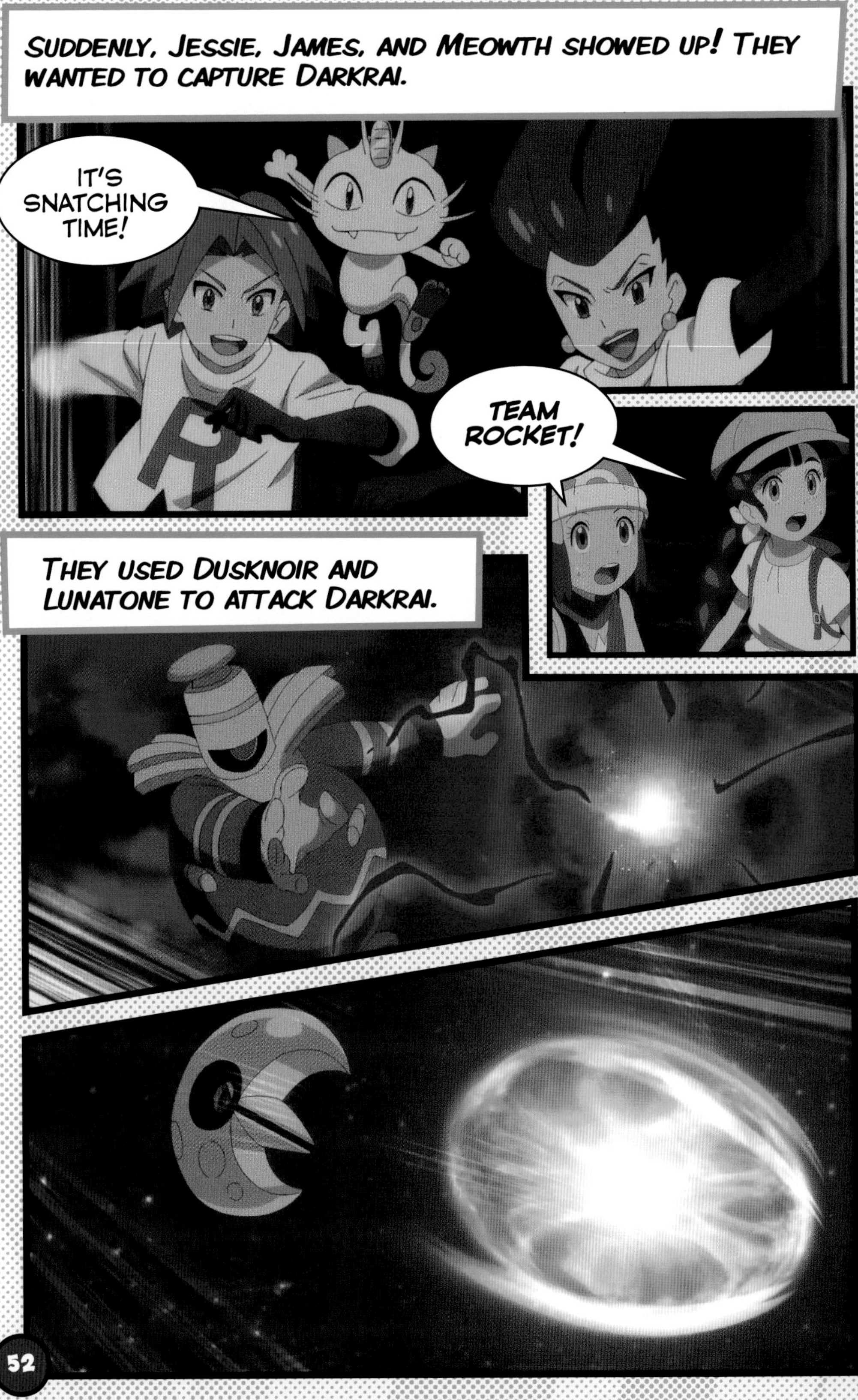
SUDDENLY, JESSIE, JAMES, AND MEOWTH SHOWED UP! THEY WANTED TO CAPTURE DARKRAI.
IT'S SNATCHING TIME!
TEAM ROCKET!
THEY USED DUSKNOIR AND LUNATONE TO ATTACK DARKRAI.

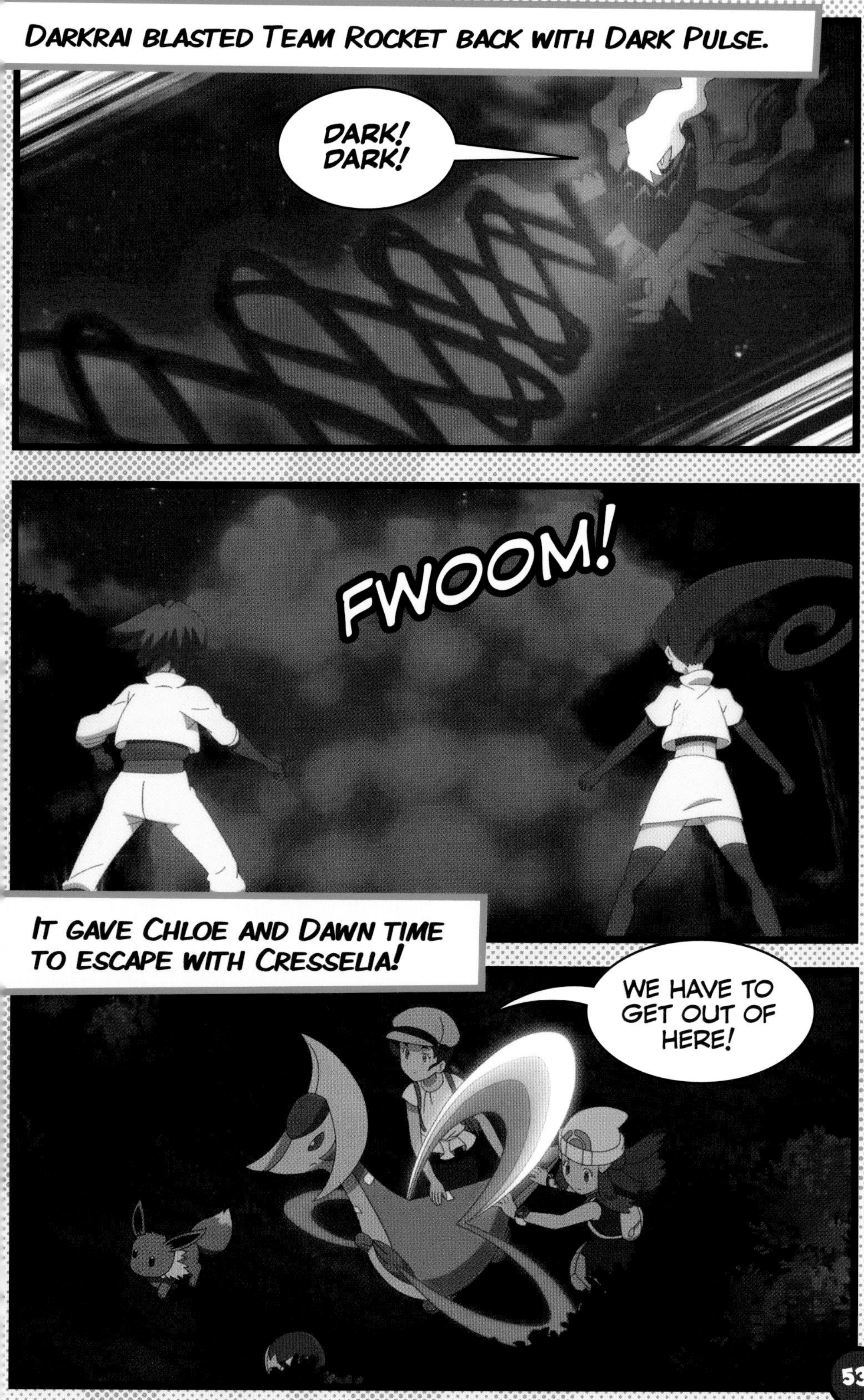
DARKRAI BLASTED TEAM ROCKET BACK WITH DARK PULSE.
DARK! DARK!
FWOOM!
IT GAVE CHLOE AND DAWN TIME TO ESCAPE WITH CRESSELIA!
WE HAVE TO GET OUT OF HERE!

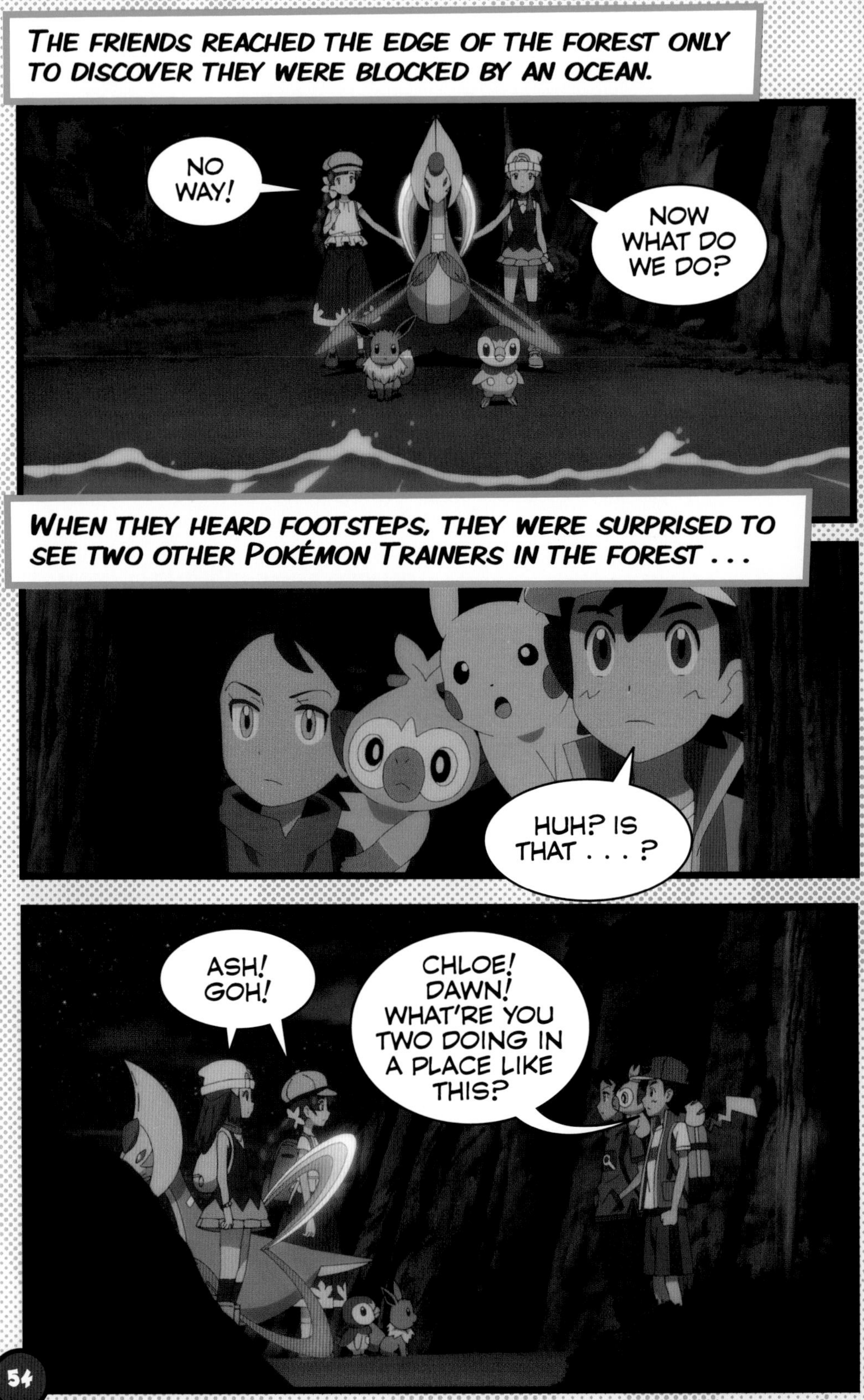
THE FRIENDS REACHED THE EDGE OF THE FOREST ONLY TO DISCOVER THEY WERE BLOCKED BY AN OCEAN.
NO WAY!
NOW WHAT DO WE DO?
WHEN THEY HEARD FOOTSTEPS, THEY WERE SURPRISED TO SEE TWO OTHER POKÉMON TRAINERS IN THE FOREST . . .
HUH? IS THAT . . . ?
ASH! GOH!
CHLOE! DAWN! WHAT'RE YOU TWO DOING IN A PLACE LIKE THIS?

ASH AND GOH EXPLAINED THAT THEY'D COME TO SINNOH BECAUSE DARKRAI WAS GIVING PEOPLE NIGHTMARES. AND CHLOE AND DAWN EXPLAINED HOW THEY FOUND THE INJURED CRESSELIA IN THE WOODS.

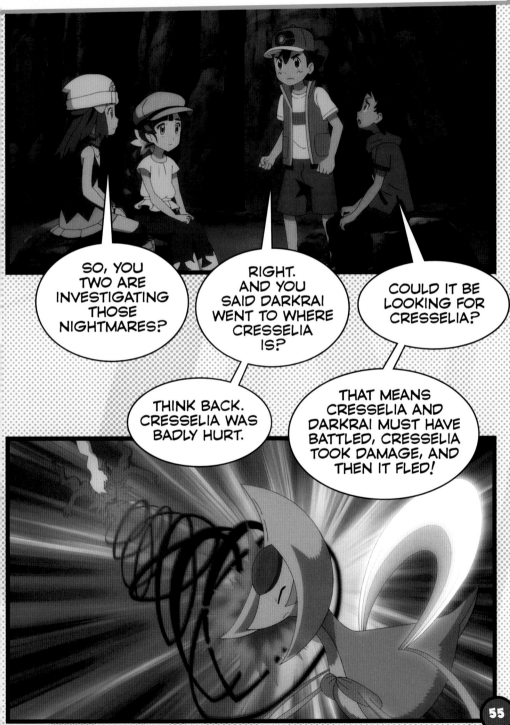

SO, YOU TWO ARE INVESTIGATING THOSE NIGHTMARES?

RIGHT. AND YOU SAID DARKRAI WENT TO WHERE CRESSELIA IS?

COULD IT BE LOOKING FOR CRESSELIA?

THINK BACK. CRESSELIA WAS BADLY HURT.

THAT MEANS CRESSELIA AND DARKRAI MUST HAVE BATTLED, CRESSELIA TOOK DAMAGE, AND THEN IT FLED!

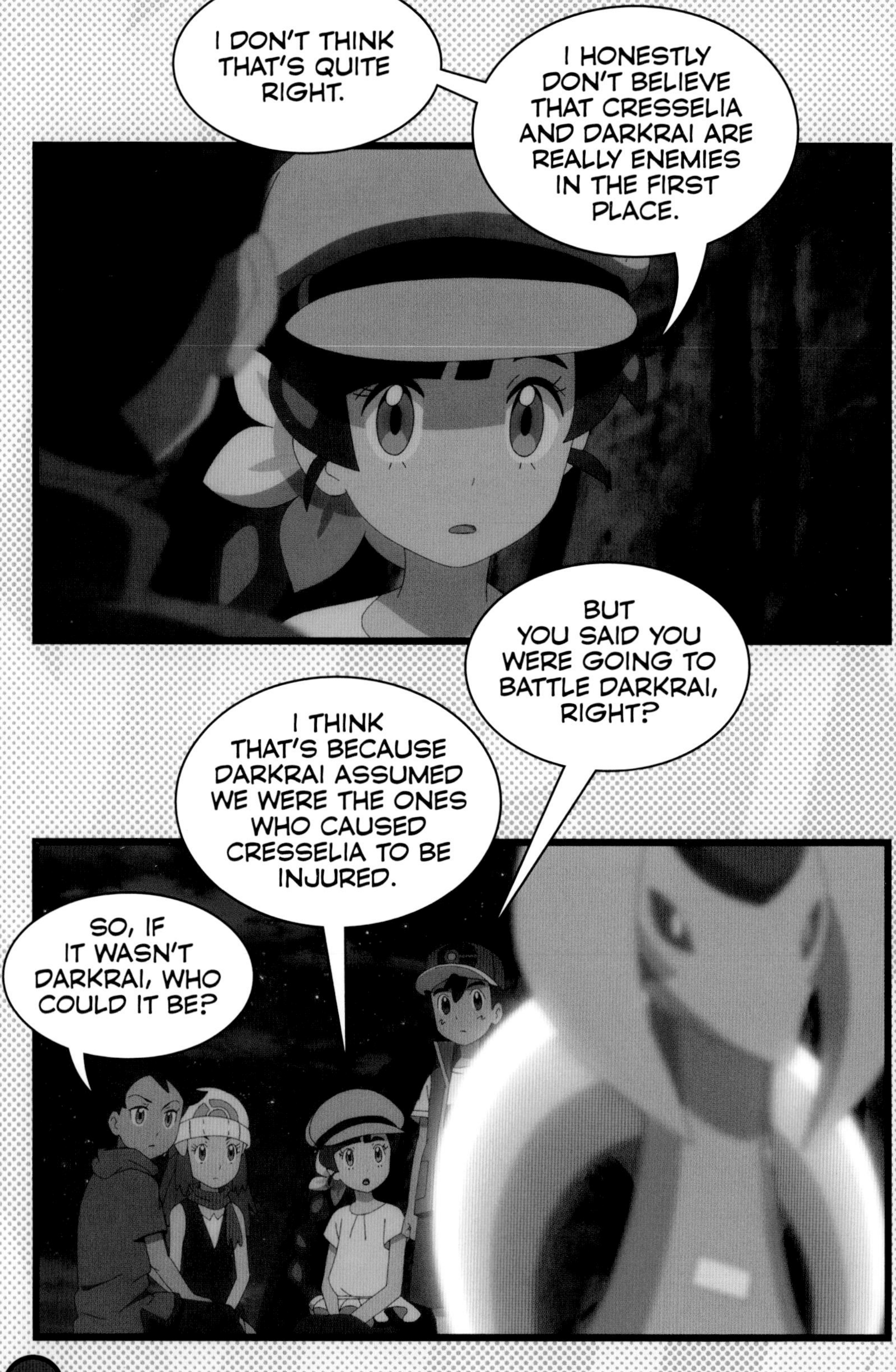
I DON'T THINK THAT'S QUITE RIGHT.
I HONESTLY DON'T BELIEVE THAT CRESSELIA AND DARKRAI ARE REALLY ENEMIES IN THE FIRST PLACE.
BUT YOU SAID YOU WERE GOING TO BATTLE DARKRAI, RIGHT?
I THINK THAT'S BECAUSE DARKRAI ASSUMED WE WERE THE ONES WHO CAUSED CRESSELIA TO BE INJURED.
SO, IF IT WASN'T DARKRAI, WHO COULD IT BE?

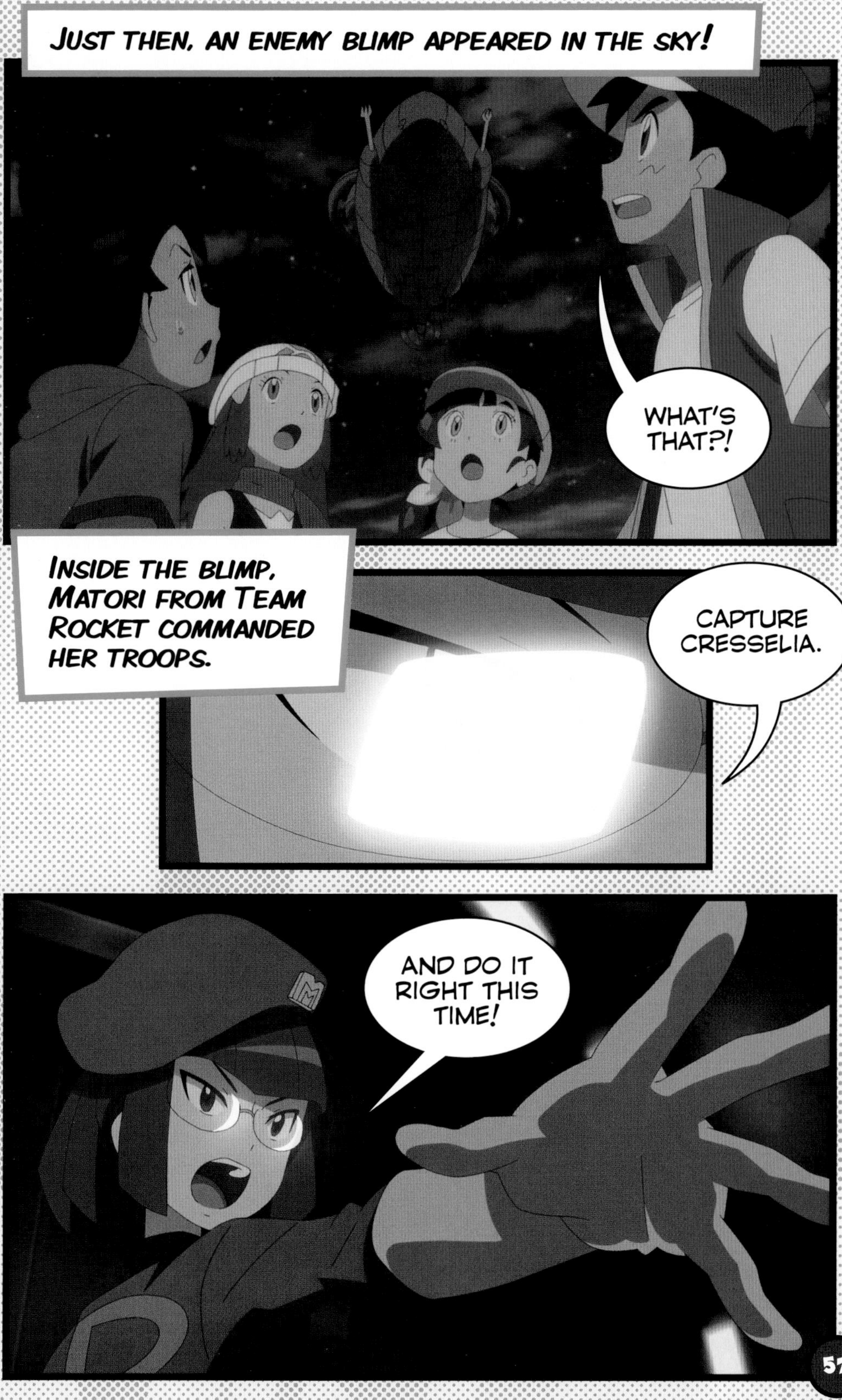
JUST THEN, AN ENEMY BLIMP APPEARED IN THE SKY!
WHAT'S THAT?!
INSIDE THE BLIMP, MATORI FROM TEAM ROCKET COMMANDED HER TROOPS.
CAPTURE CRESSELIA.
AND DO IT RIGHT THIS TIME!

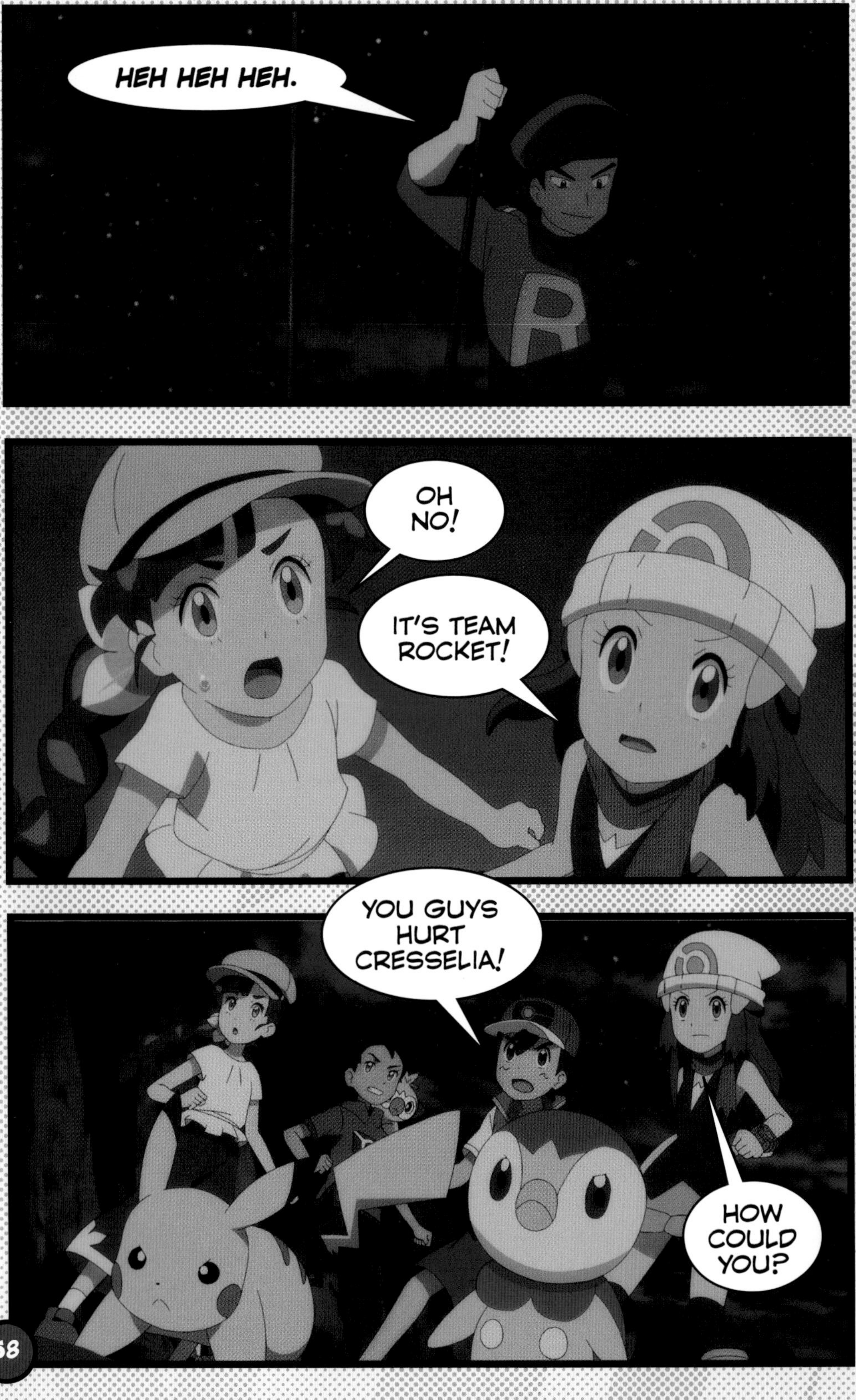
HEH HEH HEH.
OH NO!
IT'S TEAM ROCKET!
YOU GUYS HURT CRESSELIA!
HOW COULD YOU?

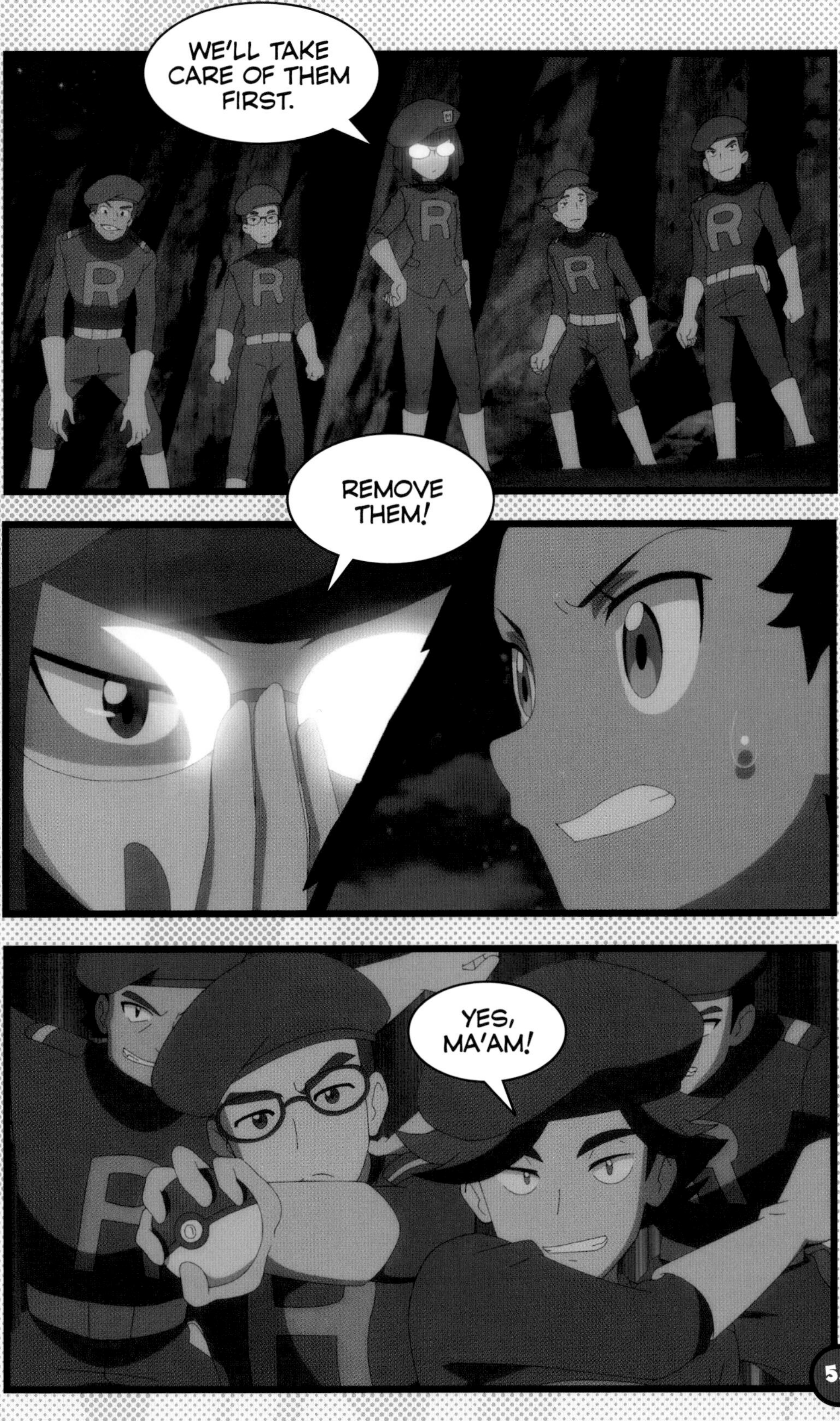
WE'LL TAKE CARE OF THEM FIRST.
REMOVE THEM!
YES, MA'AM!

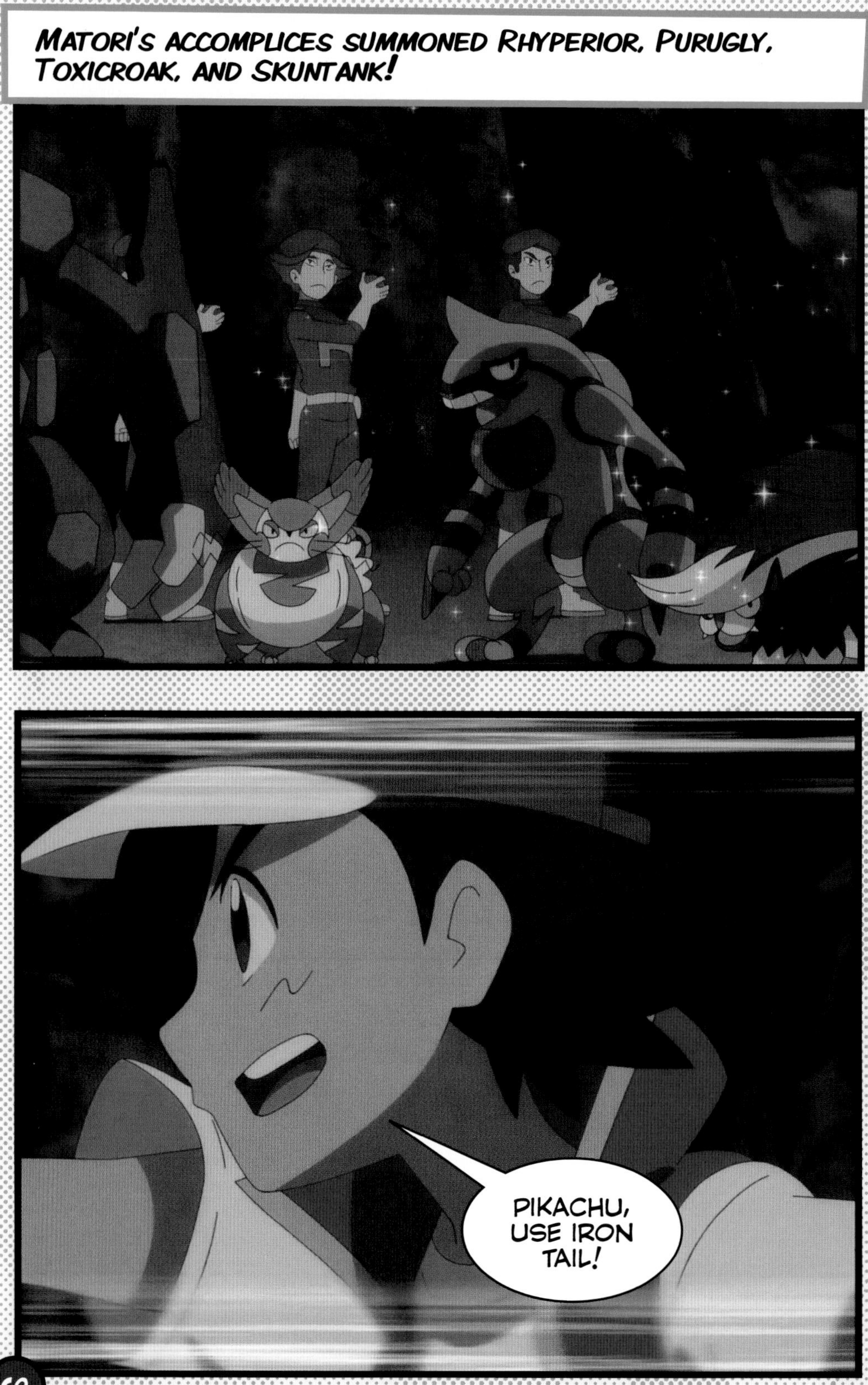
MATORI'S ACCOMPLICES SUMMONED RHYPERIOR, PURUGLY, TOXICROAK, AND SKUNTANK!
PIKACHU, USE IRON TAIL!

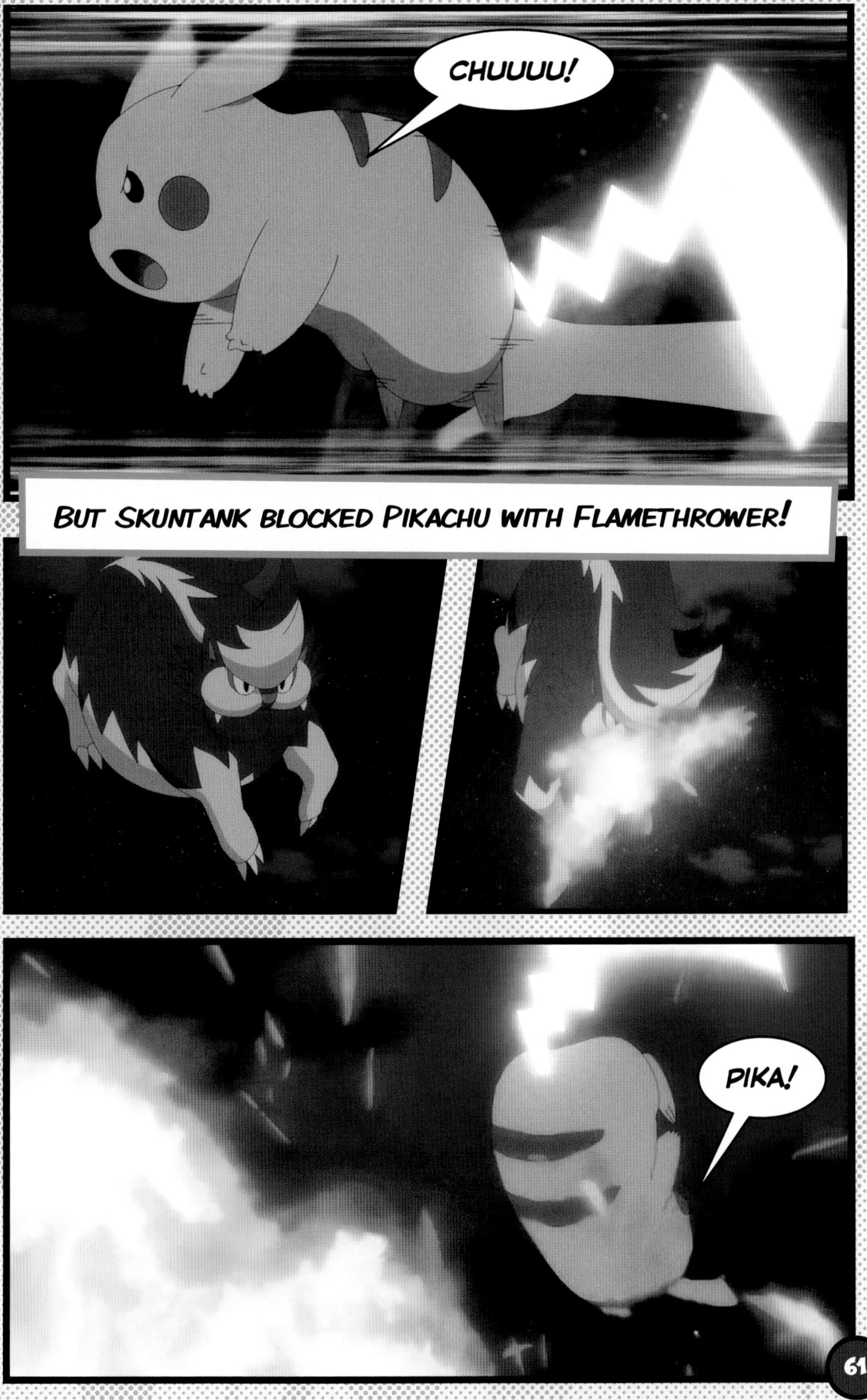
CHUUUU!
BUT SKUNTANK BLOCKED PIKACHU WITH FLAMETHROWER!
PIKA!

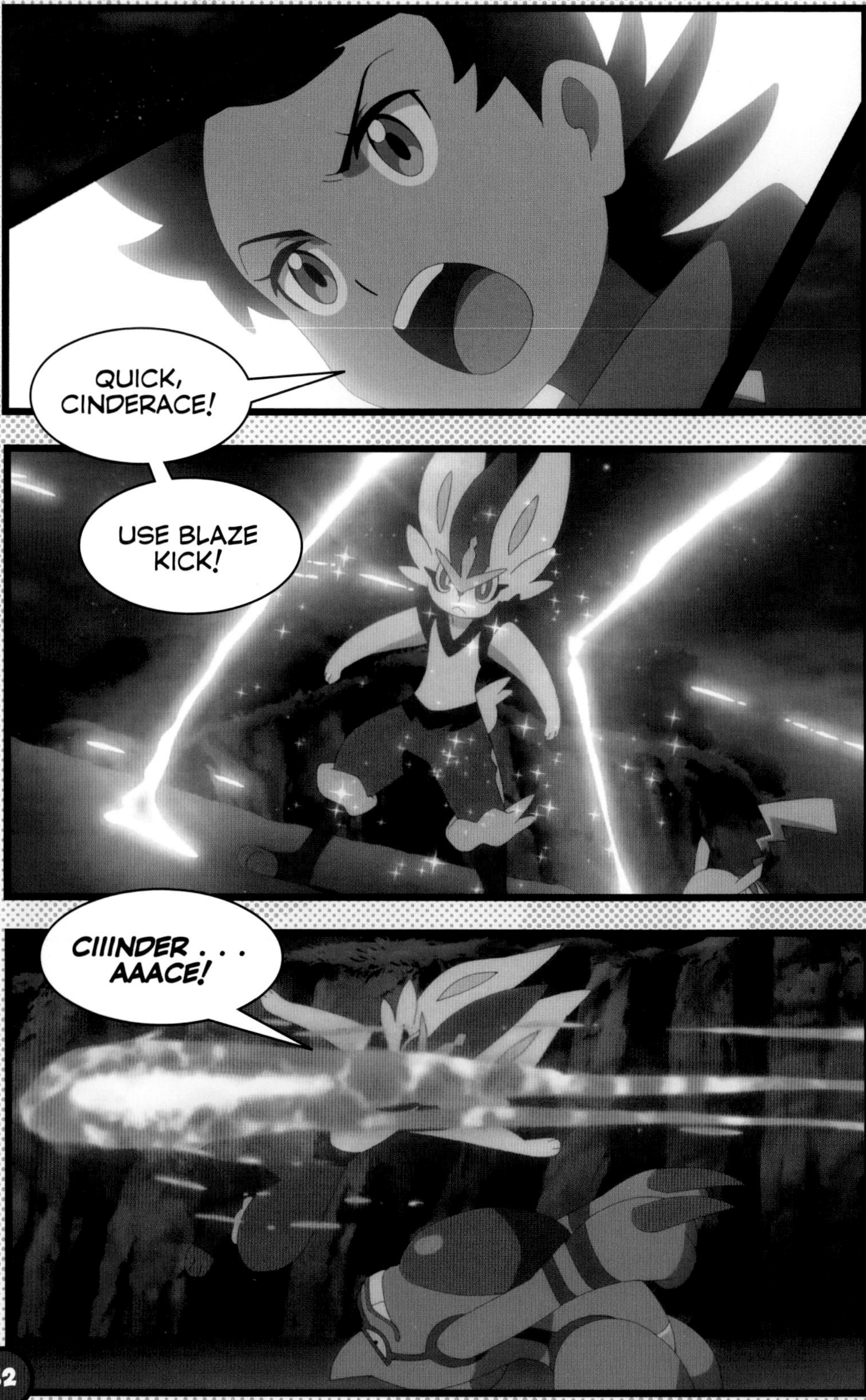
QUICK, CINDERACE!
USE BLAZE KICK!
CIIINDER . . . AAACE!

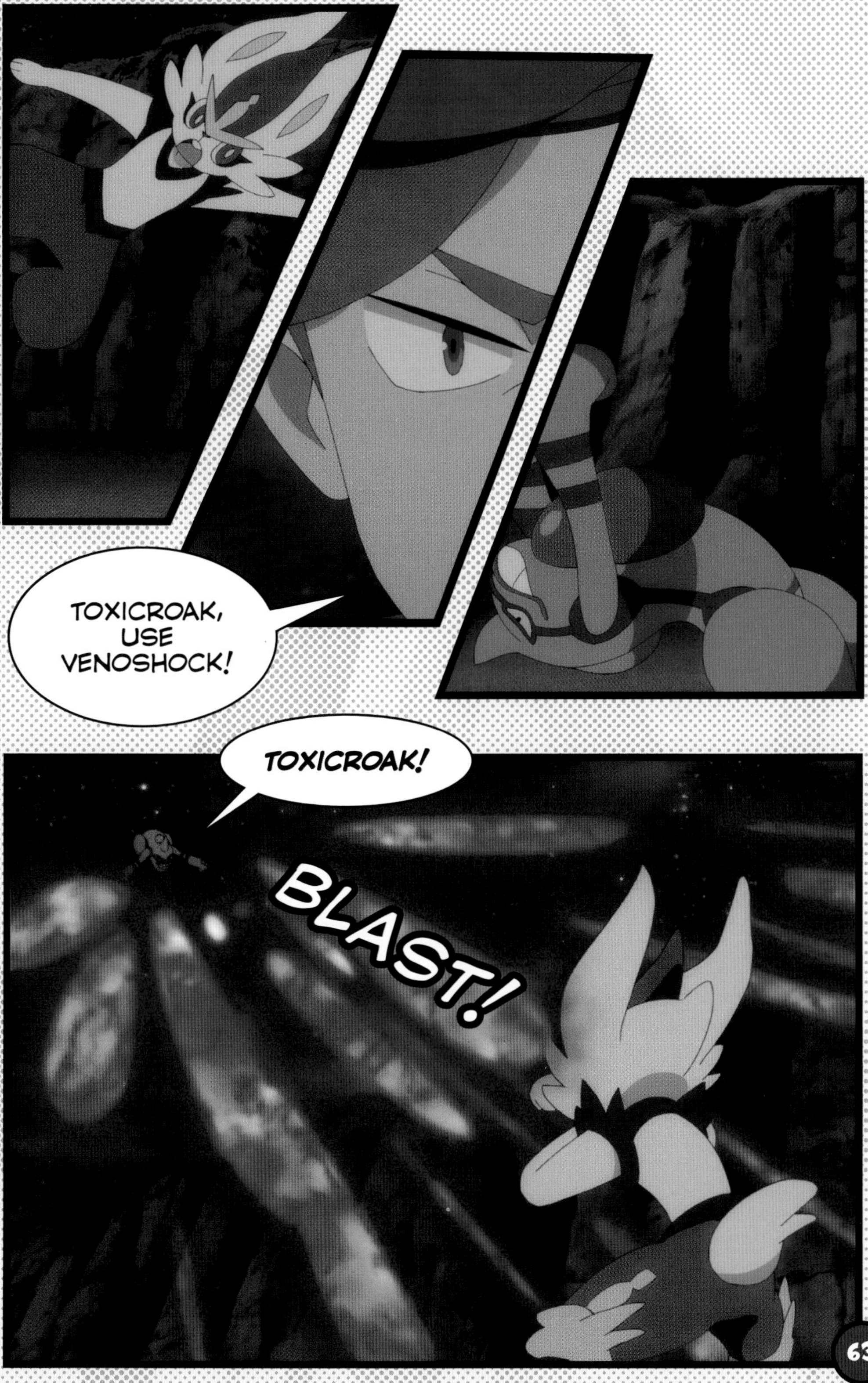
TOXICROAK, USE VENOSHOCK!
TOXICROAK!
BLAST!

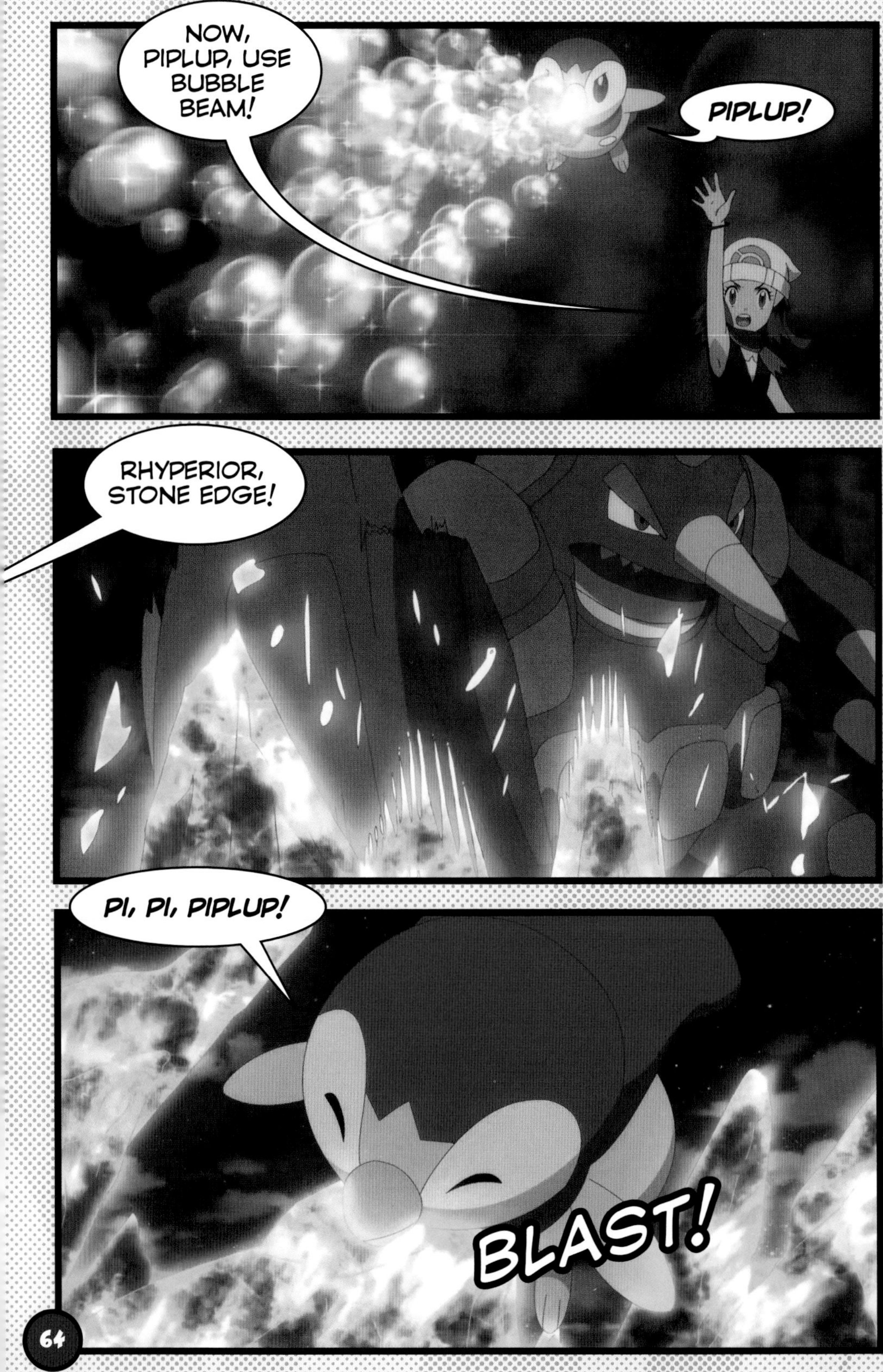
NOW, PIPLUP, USE BUBBLE BEAM!
PIPLUP!
RHYPERIOR, STONE EDGE!
PI, PI, PIPLUP!
BLAST!

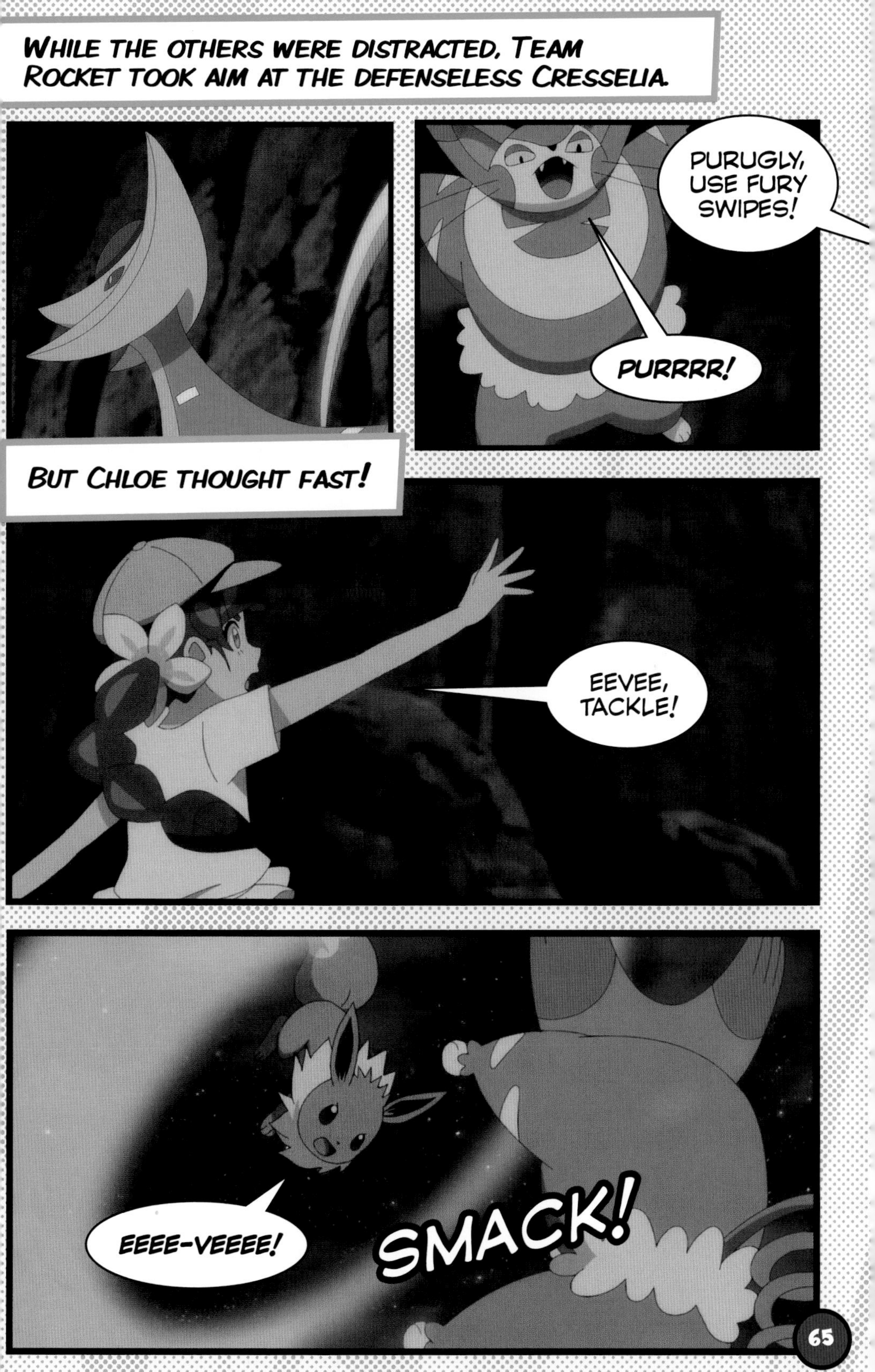
WHILE THE OTHERS WERE DISTRACTED, TEAM ROCKET TOOK AIM AT THE DEFENSELESS CRESSELIA.
PURUGLY, USE FURY SWIPES!
PURRRR!
BUT CHLOE THOUGHT FAST!
EEVEE, TACKLE!
EEEE-VEEEE!
SMACK!

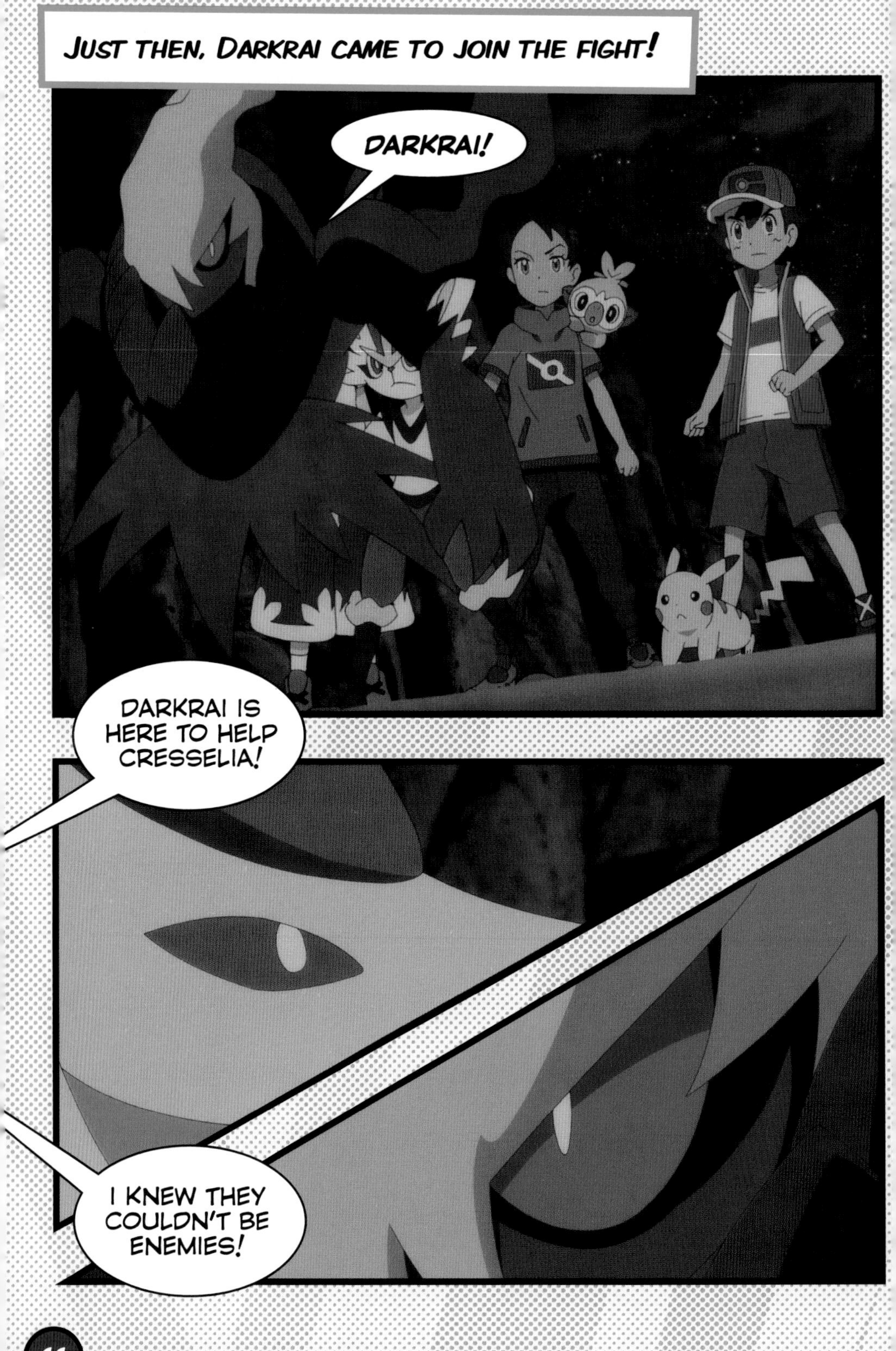
JUST THEN, DARKRAI CAME TO JOIN THE FIGHT!
DARKRAI!
DARKRAI IS HERE TO HELP CRESSELIA!
I KNEW THEY COULDN'T BE ENEMIES!

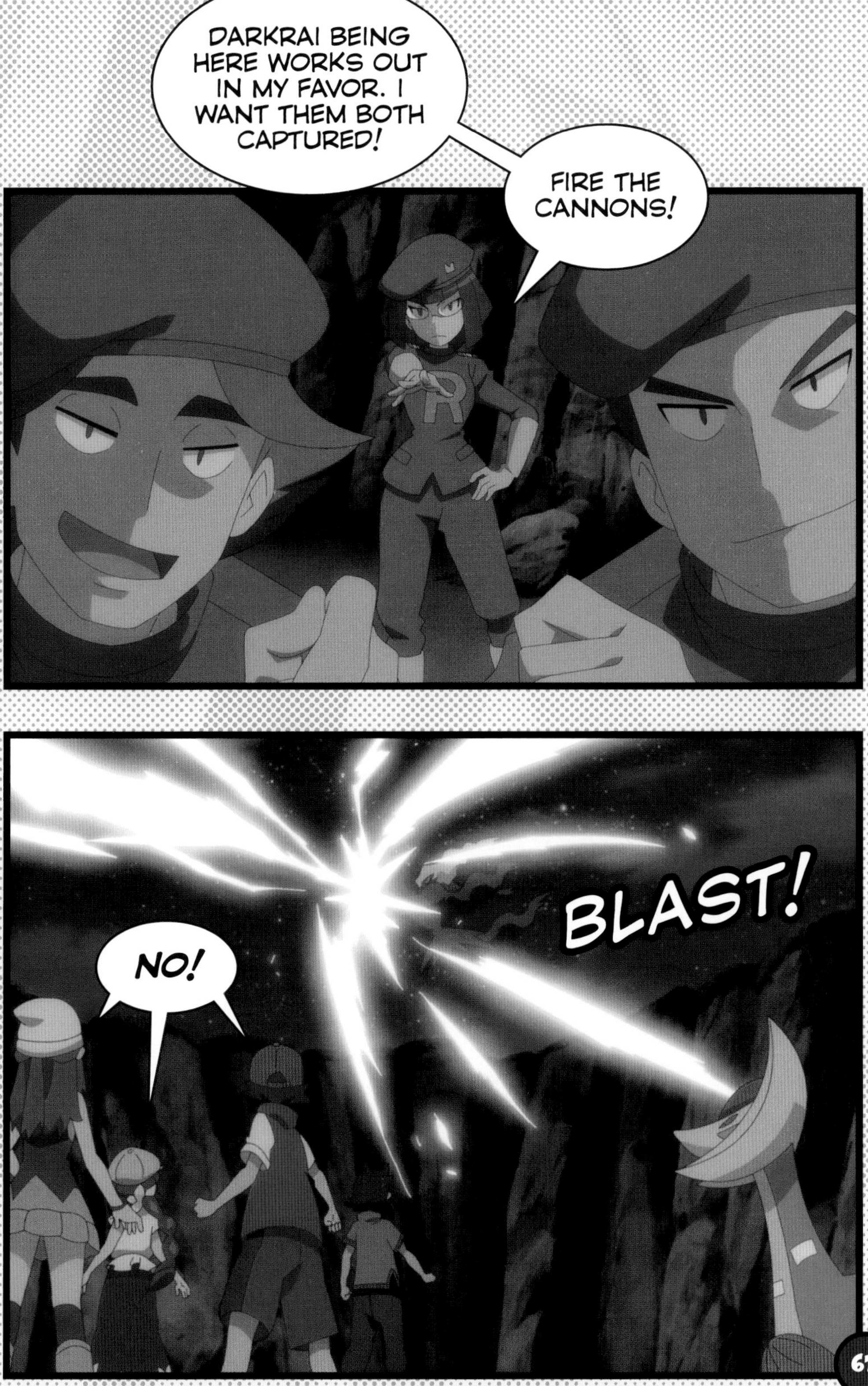
DARKRAI BEING HERE WORKS OUT IN MY FAVOR. I WANT THEM BOTH CAPTURED!
FIRE THE CANNONS!
BLAST!
NO!

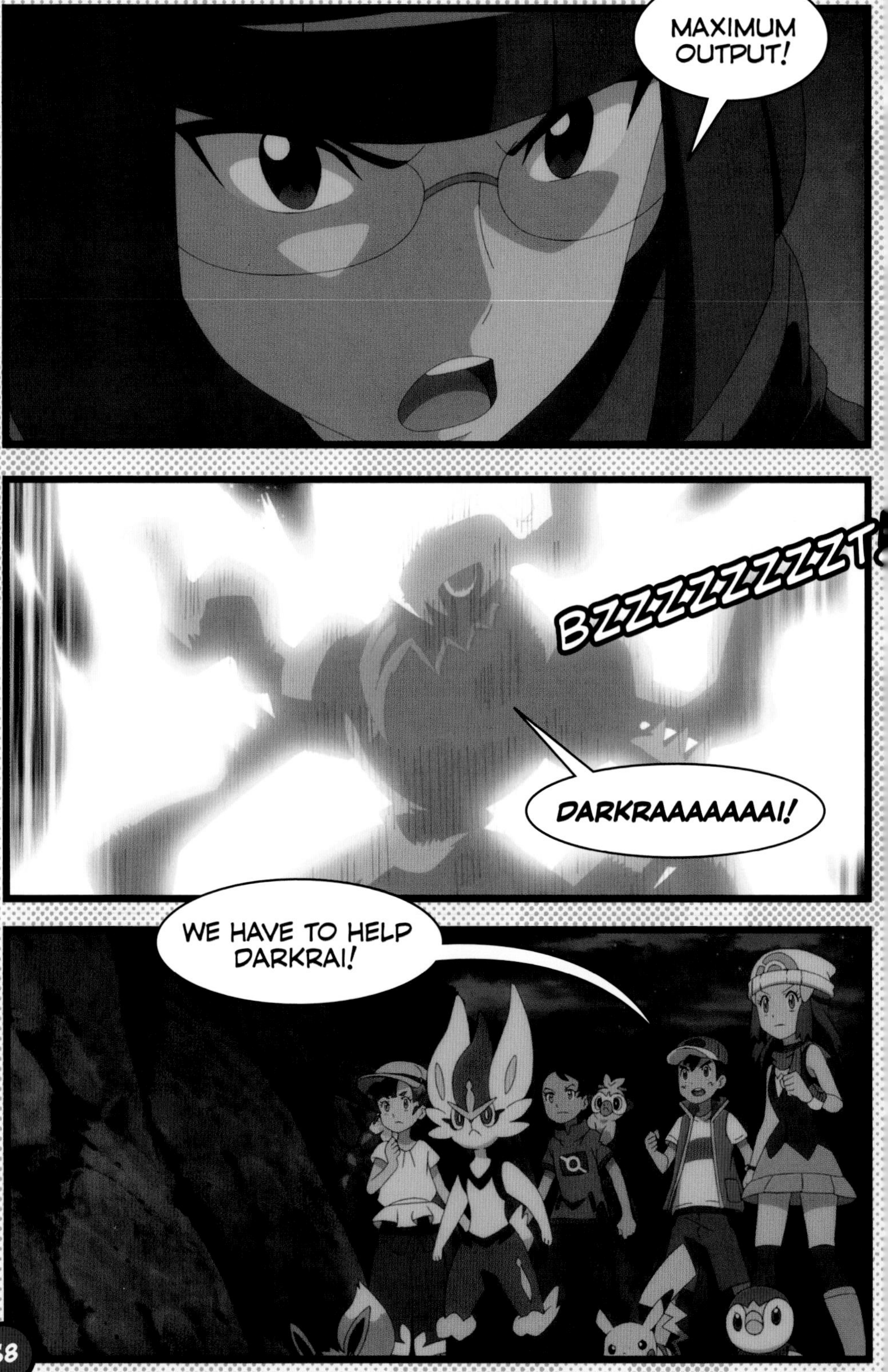
MAXIMUM OUTPUT!
BZZZZZZZZZT!
DARKRAAAAAAAI!
WE HAVE TO HELP DARKRAI!

But before the friends could reach Darkrai, Team Rocket trapped them in a net!

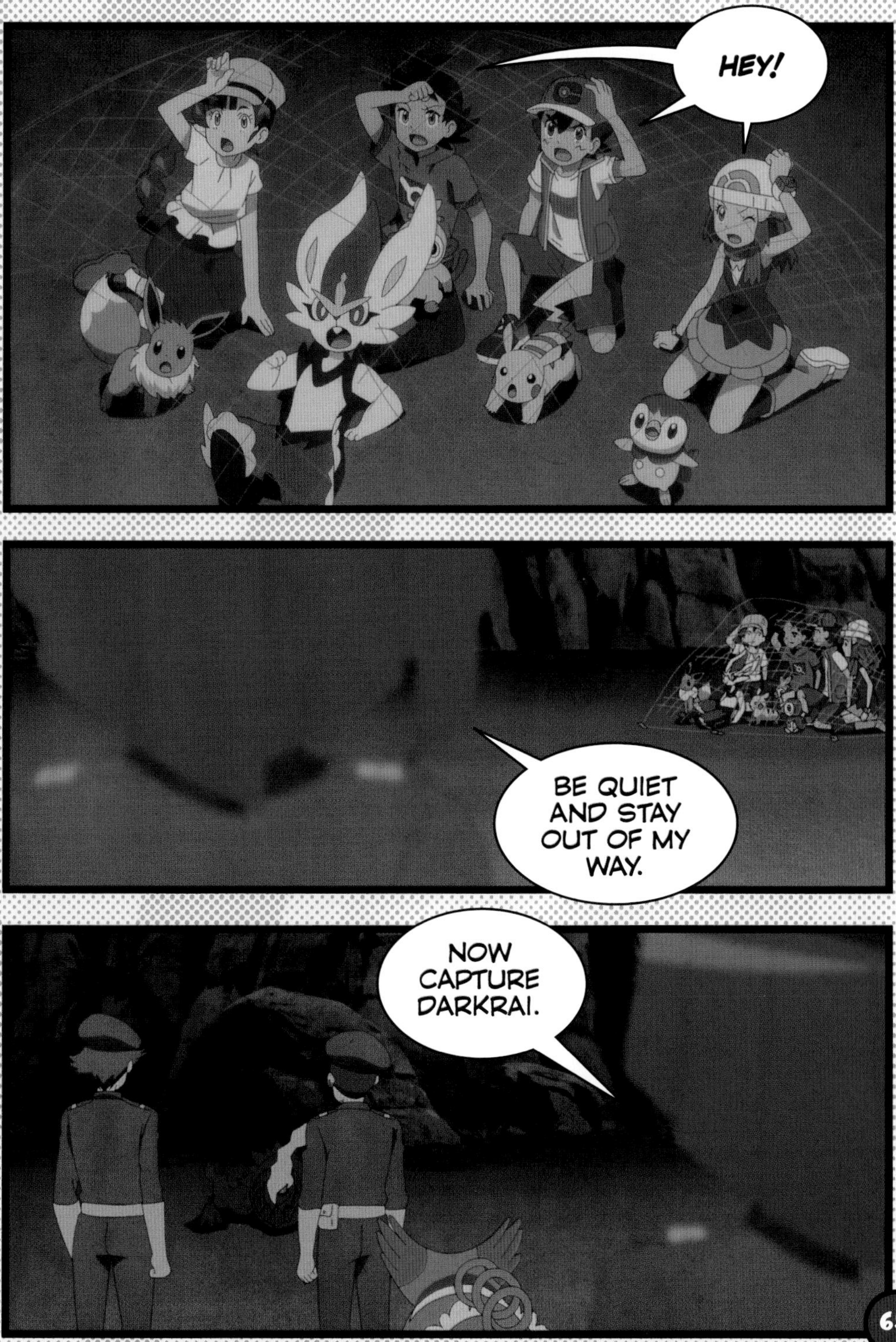
HEY!
BE QUIET AND STAY OUT OF MY WAY.
NOW CAPTURE DARKRAI.

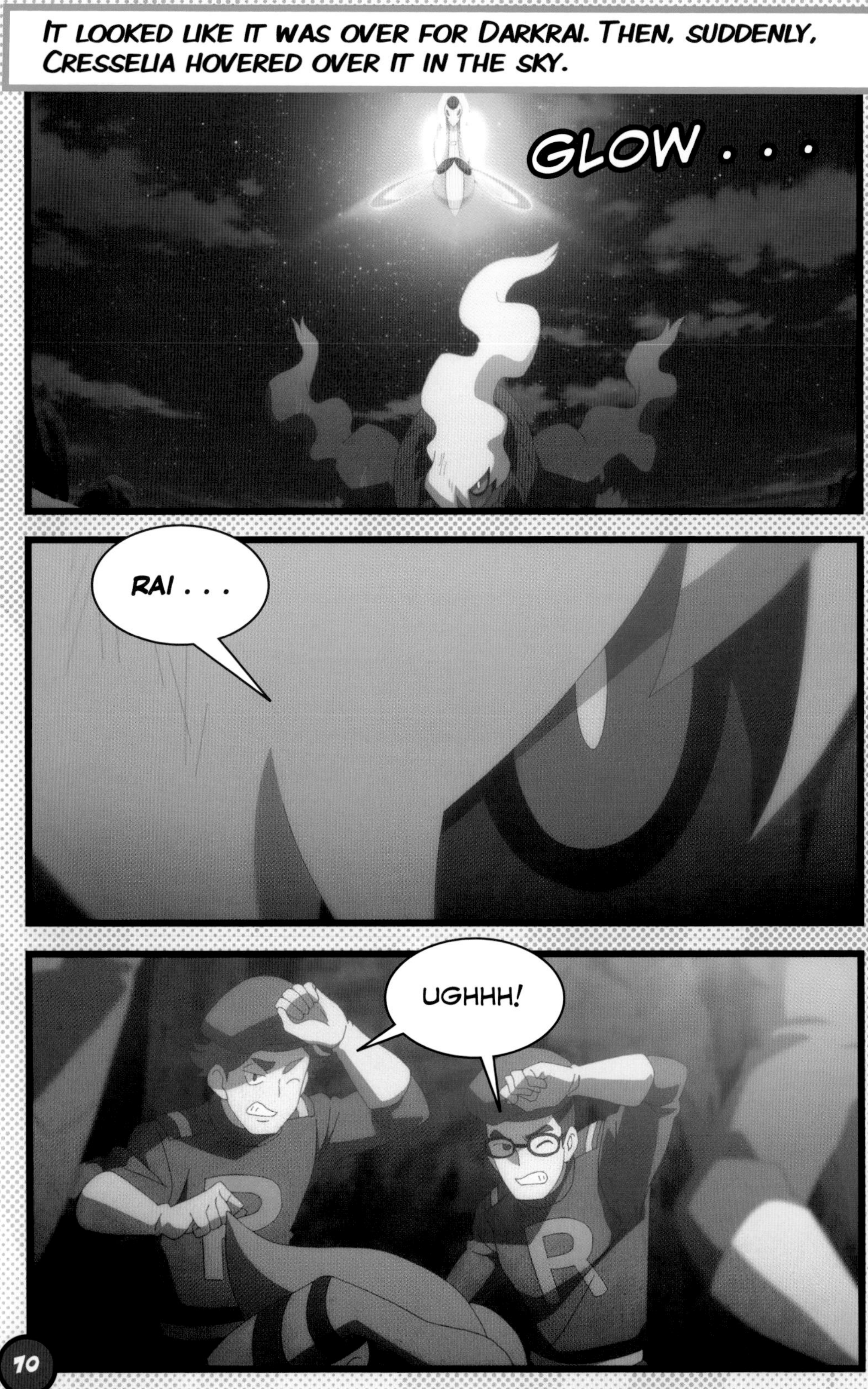
It looked like it was over for Darkrai. Then, suddenly, Cresselia hovered over it in the sky.
GLOW . . .
RAI . . .
UGHHH!

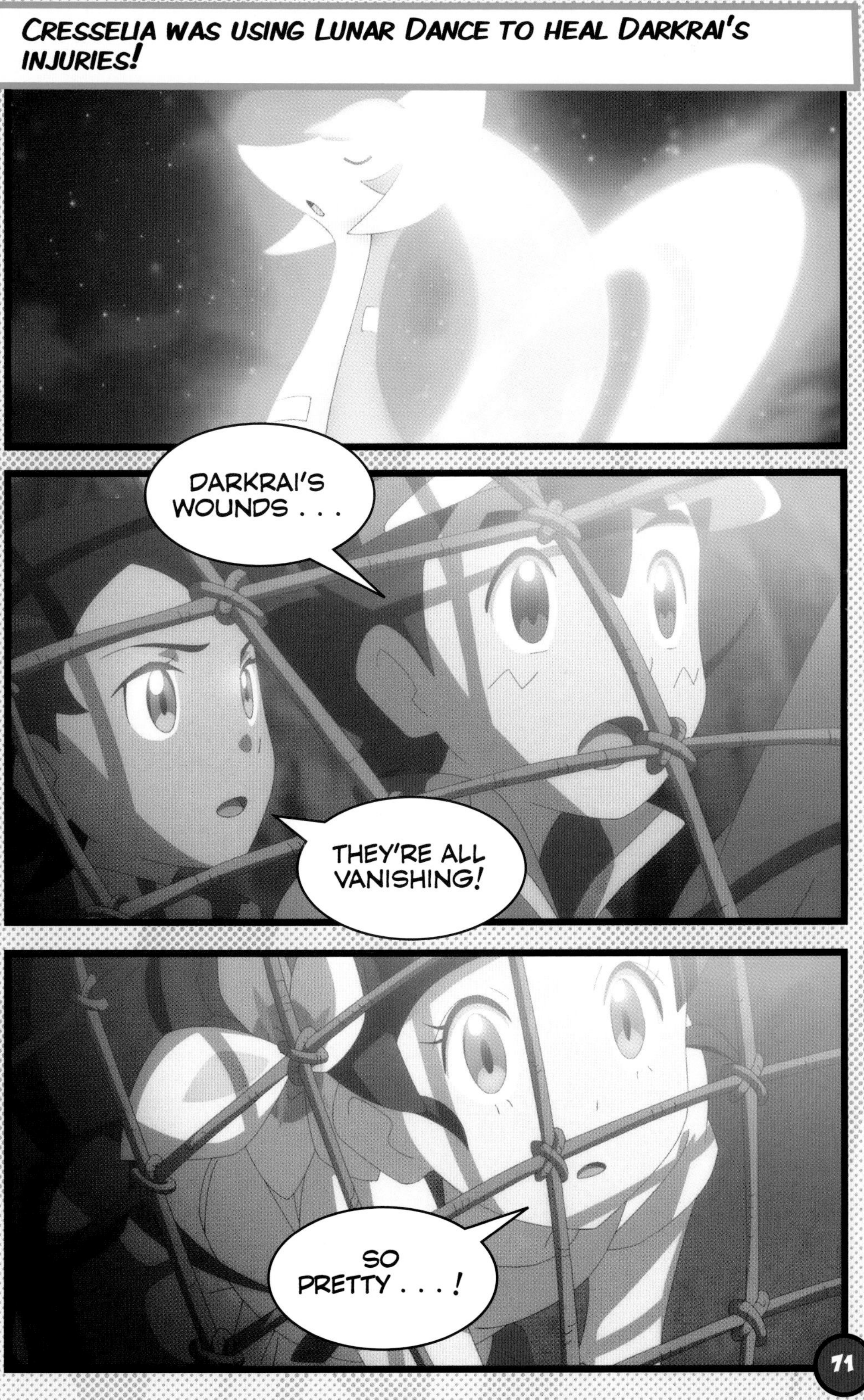
CRESSELIA WAS USING LUNAR DANCE TO HEAL DARKRAI'S INJURIES!
DARKRAI'S WOUNDS . . .
THEY'RE ALL VANISHING!
SO PRETTY . . . !

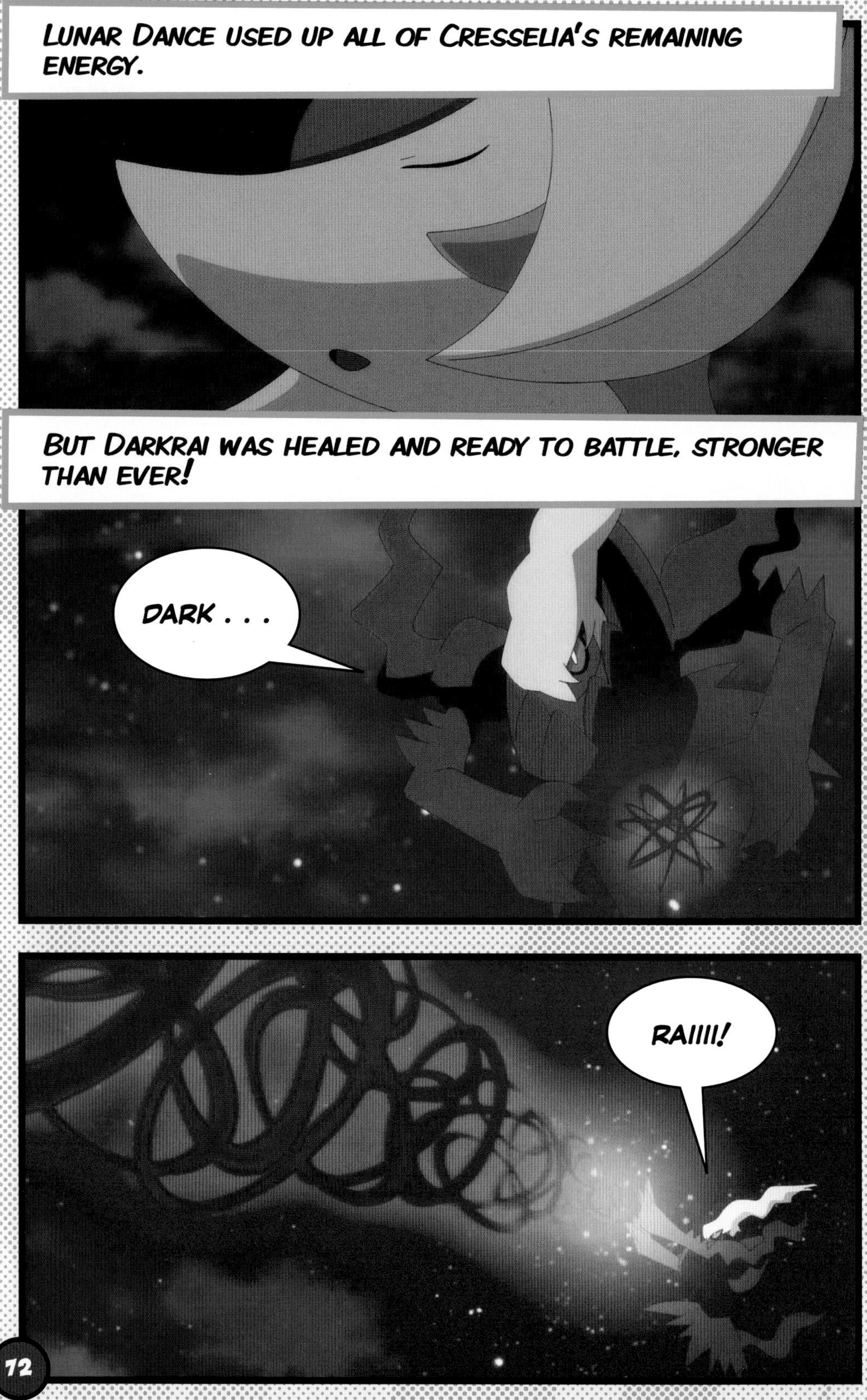
LUNAR DANCE USED UP ALL OF CRESSELIA'S REMAINING ENERGY.
BUT DARKRAI WAS HEALED AND READY TO BATTLE, STRONGER THAN EVER!
DARK . . .
RAIIII!

Its powerful Shadow Pulse destroyed Matori's blimp!

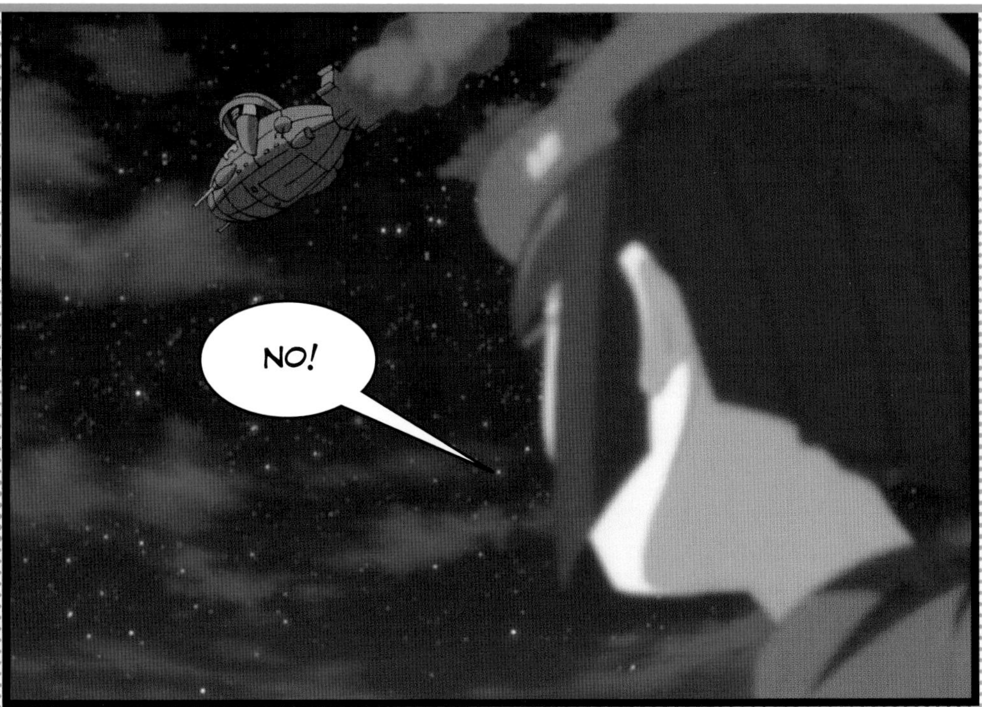
NO!

Then Darkrai powered up Dark Void.

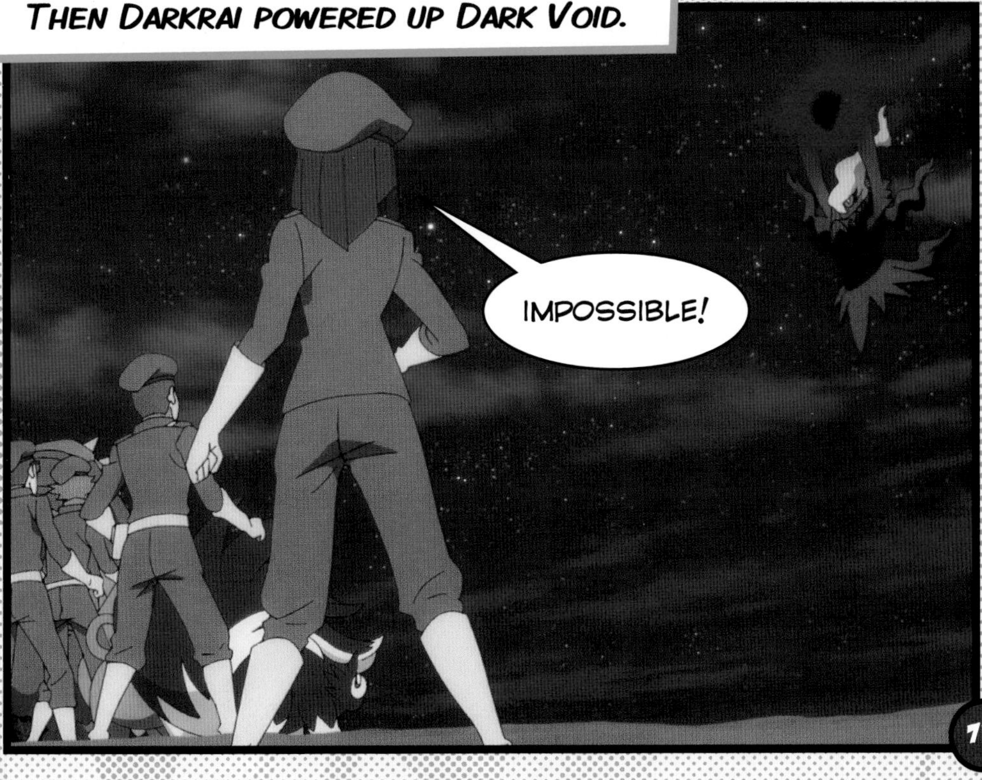
IMPOSSIBLE!

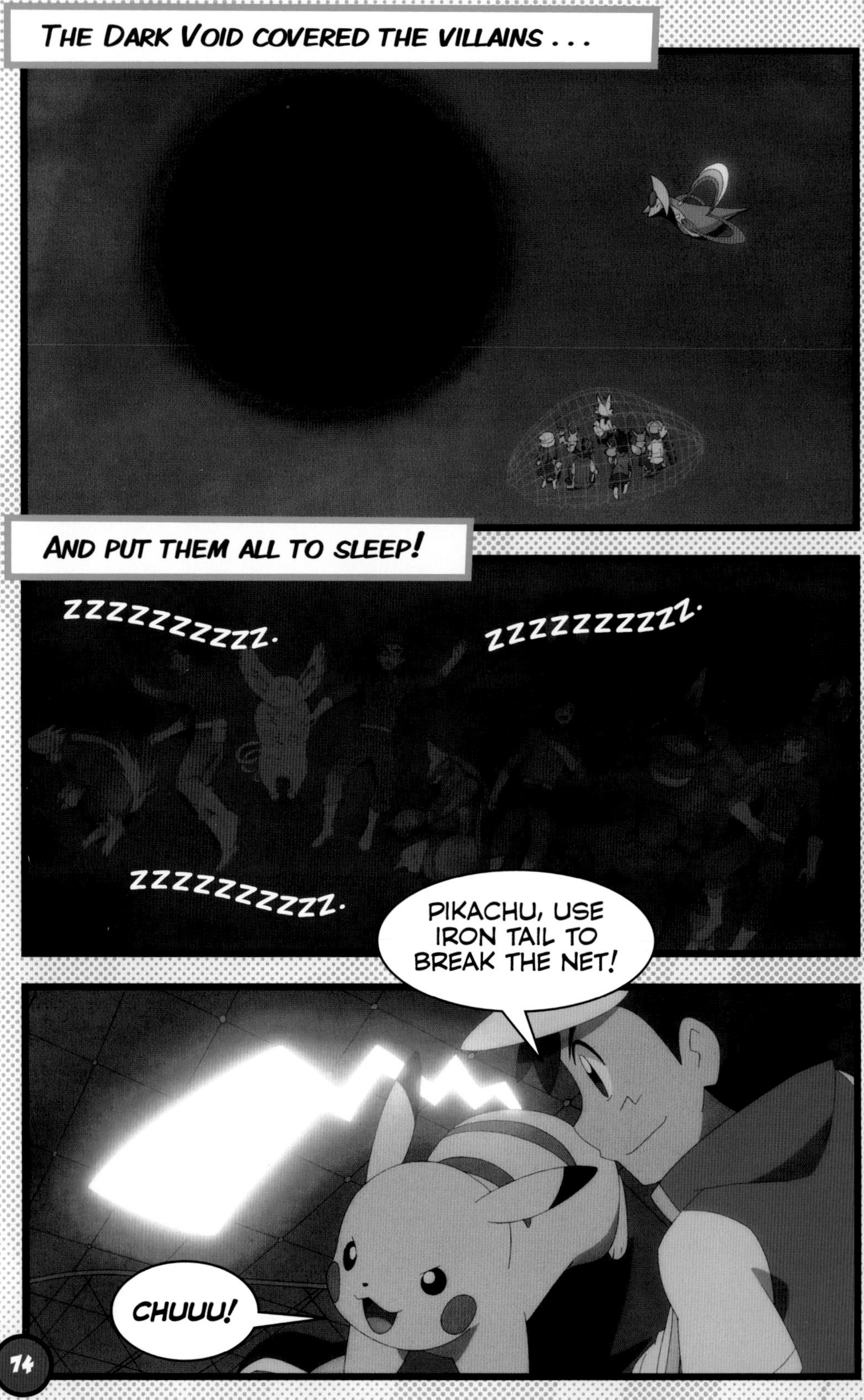
THE DARK VOID COVERED THE VILLAINS . . .
AND PUT THEM ALL TO SLEEP!
ZZZZZZZZZZZ.
ZZZZZZZZZZZ.
ZZZZZZZZZZZ.
PIKACHU, USE IRON TAIL TO BREAK THE NET!
CHUUU!

THE FRIENDS WERE SAFE, BUT CRESSELIA WAS DANGEROUSLY WEAK.

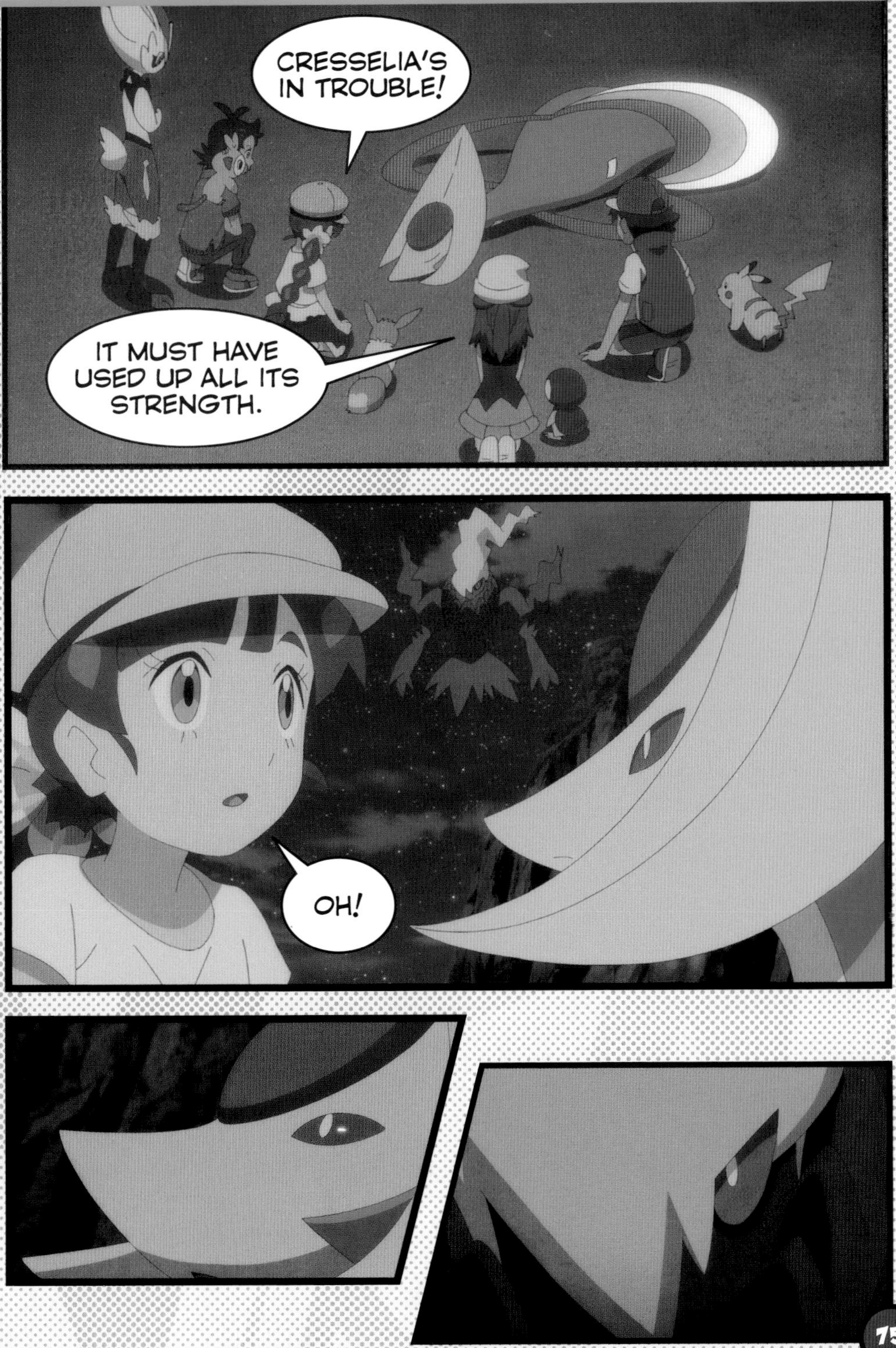
CRESSELIA'S IN TROUBLE!
IT MUST HAVE USED UP ALL ITS STRENGTH.
OH!

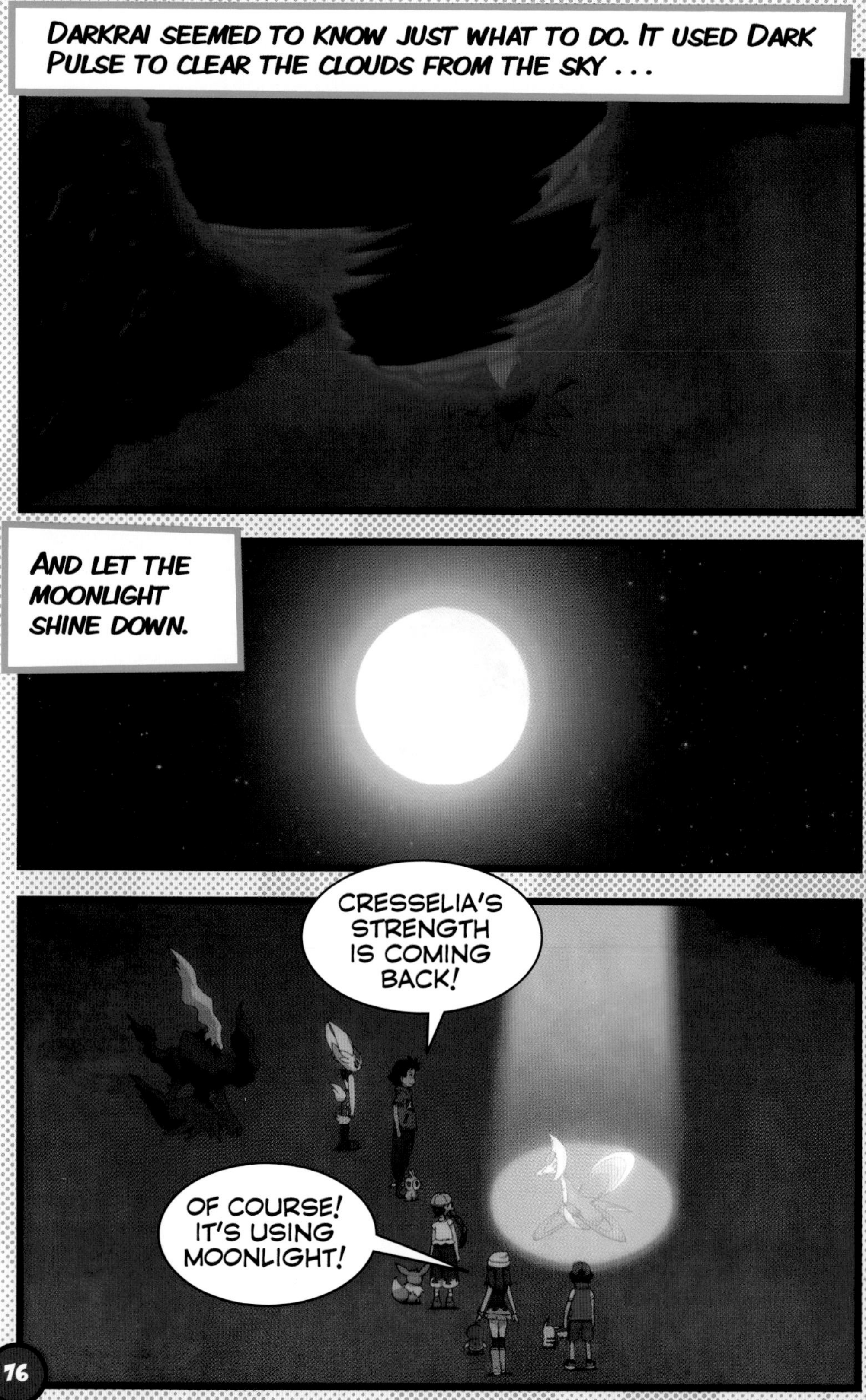
DARKRAI SEEMED TO KNOW JUST WHAT TO DO. IT USED DARK PULSE TO CLEAR THE CLOUDS FROM THE SKY . . .
AND LET THE MOONLIGHT SHINE DOWN.
CRESSELIA'S STRENGTH IS COMING BACK!
OF COURSE! IT'S USING MOONLIGHT!

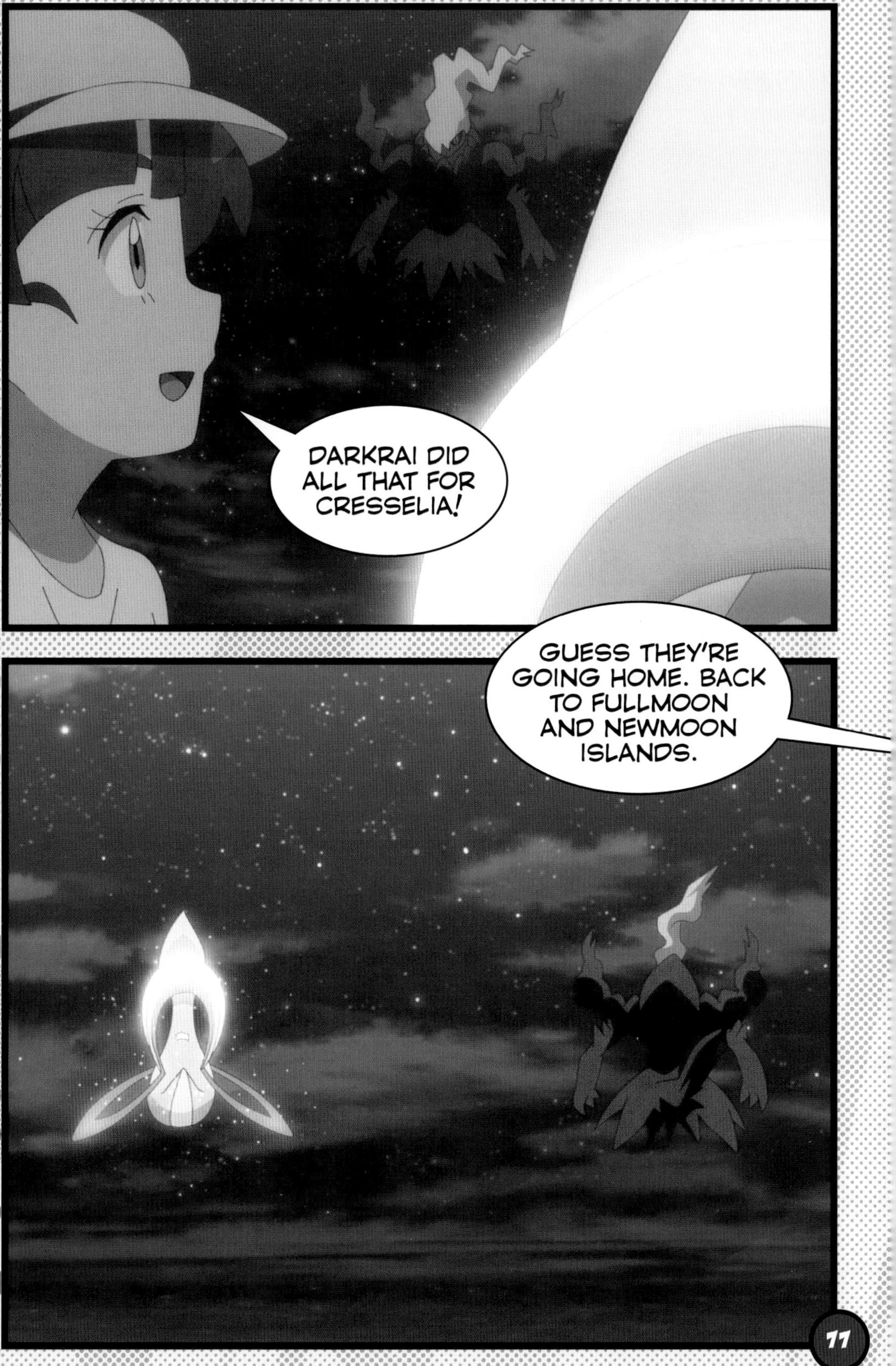
DARKRAI DID ALL THAT FOR CRESSELIA!
GUESS THEY'RE GOING HOME. BACK TO FULLMOON AND NEWMOON ISLANDS.

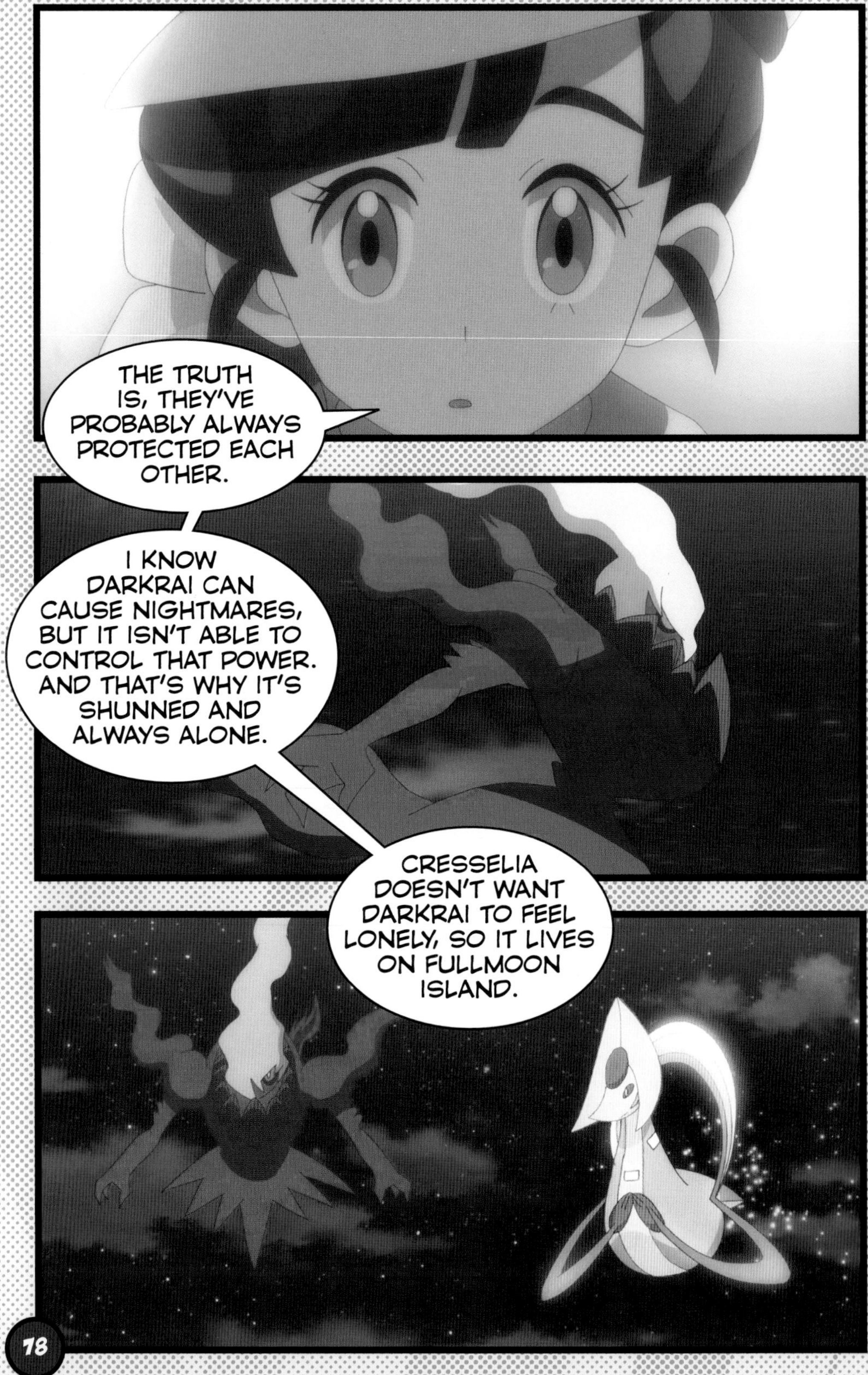
THE TRUTH IS, THEY'VE PROBABLY ALWAYS PROTECTED EACH OTHER.
I KNOW DARKRAI CAN CAUSE NIGHTMARES, BUT IT ISN'T ABLE TO CONTROL THAT POWER. AND THAT'S WHY IT'S SHUNNED AND ALWAYS ALONE.
CRESSELIA DOESN'T WANT DARKRAI TO FEEL LONELY, SO IT LIVES ON FULLMOON ISLAND.

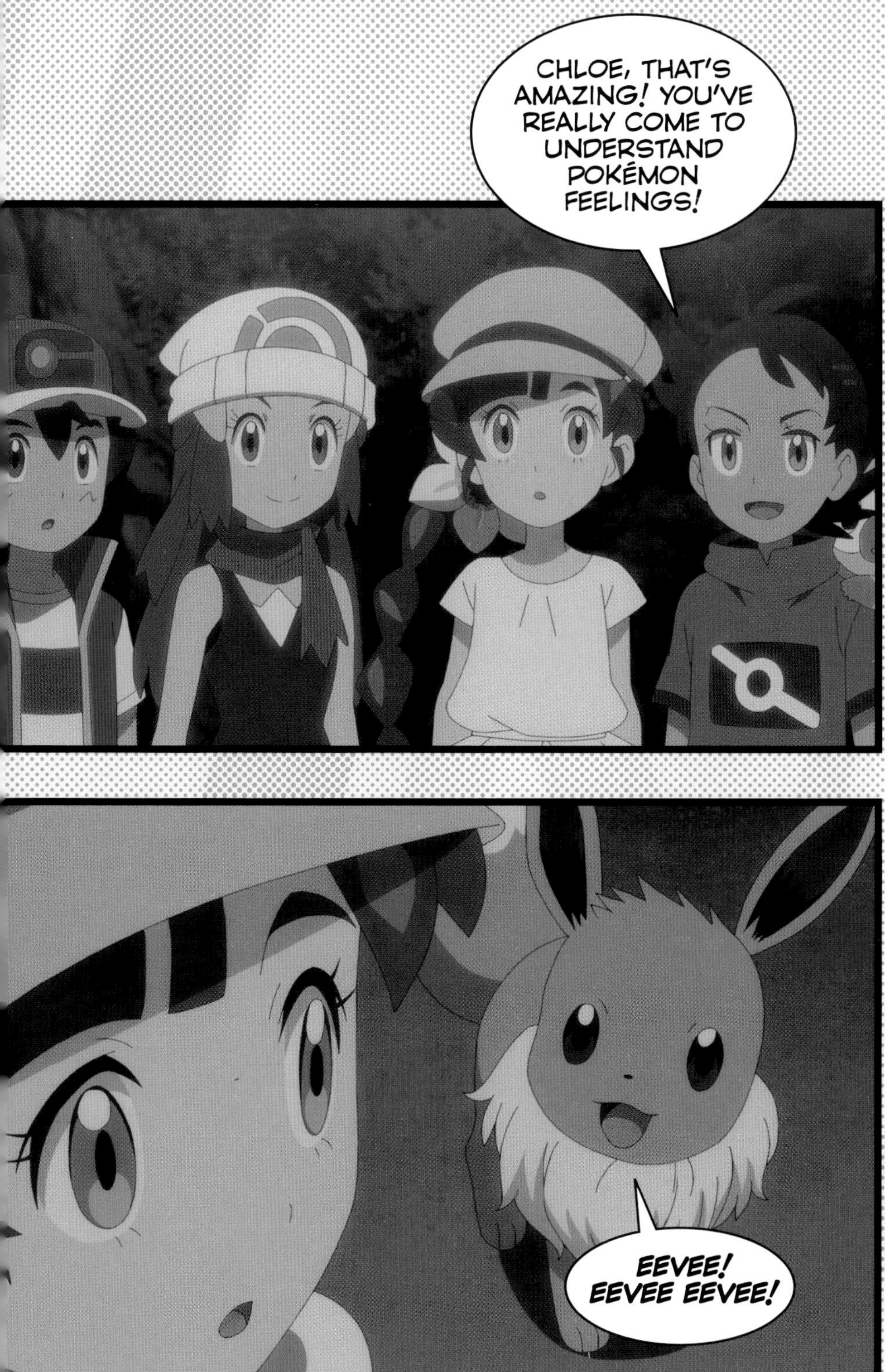
CHLOE, THAT'S AMAZING! YOU'VE REALLY COME TO UNDERSTAND POKÉMON FEELINGS!
EEVEE! EEVEE EEVEE!

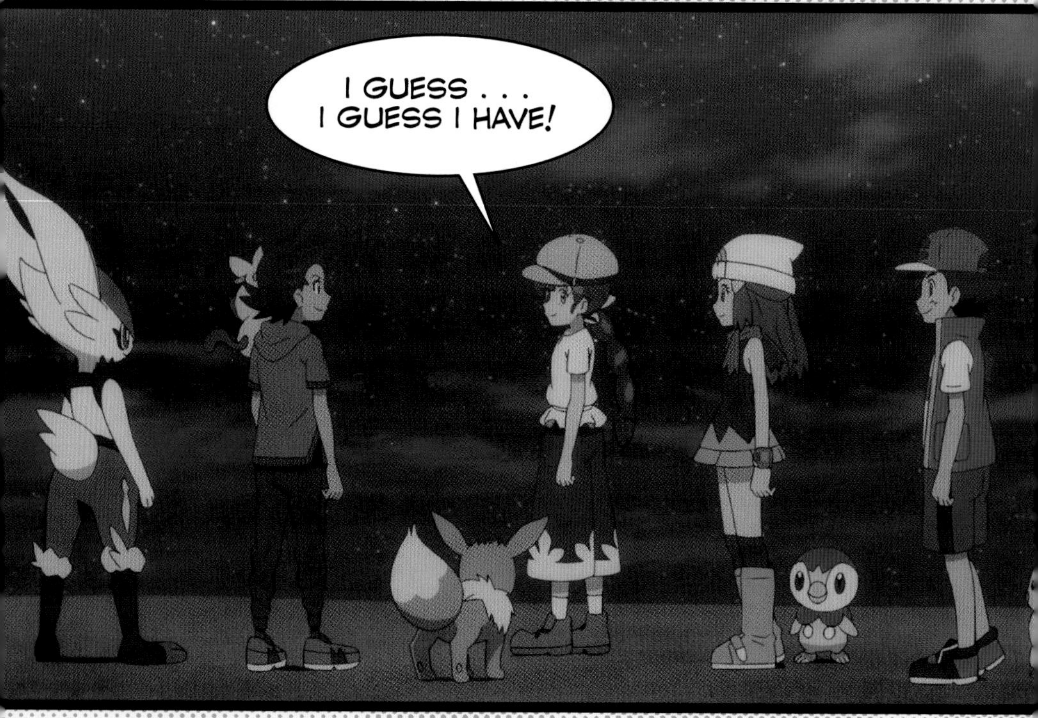
I GUESS . . . I GUESS I HAVE!

Chloe, Dawn, Ash, and Goh had strengthened bonds and explored mysteries with their Pokémon in Sinnoh. And by trusting herself and showing Darkrai and Cresselia what was in her heart, Chloe discovered she was following the exact right path on her Pokémon journey!